"Please!" Her _____ _____ mattered at the _____ _____ _____ arm again. "Please, n_____ _____ _____ out of here, get me hom_____

This is what come_____ _____ involved. The Owl is no white knig_____ _____ e the girl a sour look as the whine o_____ _____ stant sirens began approaching.

"Getting out of here is just what I had in mind," I grumbled. "If you can keep up, come on."

She gave it a good try. Fortunately for her, the current vogue in women's footwear was a type of colourful sneaker. She'd never have kept the pace in heels.

We beat it down back alleys in a south-easterly direction until we hit Fountain, where I flagged a passing independent cab. He had no radio, so I figured we'd be safe for the moment.

"Sixth and Main, downtown," I said, choosing a direction at random.

The wind blew dust and red dirt against the glass with a soft, spattering noise. I looked away, at the sudden and unwanted companion I had so unfortunately acquired. She was still gulping in hysteria and gasping for breath, half-collapsed against the cheap vinyl seat. Obviously, she was in no condition for questioning, but the Owl is a less than kind person. It ruffles my feathers a tad when I have to shoot people without knowing why.

"What's your name, girl?"

"Scarlet," she panted. "Scarlet Serenade."

Also by the same author,
and available from NEL:

The Owl

The Owl 2
Scarlet Serenade

Bob Forward

NEW ENGLISH LIBRARY
Hodder and Stoughton

First published in Great
Britain in 1990 by New
English Library Paperbacks

A New English Library
paperback original

Printed and bound in Great Britain
for Hodder and Stoughton
Paperbacks, a division of Hodder
and Stoughton Ltd., Mill Road,
Dunton Green, Sevenoaks, Kent,
TN13 2YA. (Editorial Office:
47 Bedford Square, London
WC1B 3DP) by Cox & Wyman.
Photoset by Chippendale Type,
Otley, West Yorkshire.

British Library C.I.P.

Forward, Bob
  Scarlet serenade.
  I. Title
  823'.914[F]

  ISBN 0–450–53215–1

There's a wind in Los Angeles that blows maybe twice a year. It comes from the east, hot and arid, straight from the sandy hell of Mojave itself.

The natives call it the Santa Ana, and with it comes madness. The man doesn't live who can entirely escape the hair-trigger insanity borne on the hot winds from the east. The blowing dust is a constant irritant, a nagging devil that never lets up. It makes your eyes water and your nose bleed, and it goes on for four or five days without a single pause.

The first day it makes you a little irritable.

By the fifth, you're ready to kill somebody.

The cops say that there are three nights to watch out for – Fridays, full moons, and Santa Anas. Anyone with a loose screw – and there are a lot of them in L.A. – becomes completely unhinged on those nights. The cops have their hands full.

Sometimes you get all three at once. A hot, drunk Friday night, with the full moon turned blood-red from the blowing desert in the howling sky. It is then that even the most rational citizen begins to hear the demons in his head . . . the ones that whisper the joys of bloodshed, the insane satisfaction of a violent eruption, the wild delight of a blunt instrument, a slashing knife, or a thundering firearm. The wind sings a bloodsong to the beast in men.

A soft, scarlet serenade to the fearful fascination that is murder.

MONDAY

1

You could sort of tell it was going to be a bad week. It was Monday, and the air was hot and deathly still. A sort of sullen tension hung in the atmosphere, blanketing all of Hollywood with a feeling of dread anticipation.

The wind was coming.

You could feel it, all right. Like an impending bar fight, the Santa Ana wind never arrives without plenty of warning.

And like an impending bar fight, there wasn't a damn thing to be done about it. You just had to grit your teeth and ride it through.

I was walking up Highland, heading north, going no place in particular. Just moving. Always moving. To my right, a bum slept fitfully in the afternoon heat, curled up in the shade of an alley dumpster. The bum snorted and twitched in his sleep, unhappily pulling at his collar. Even in his sleep he felt the wind coming – and he didn't like it.

Stopping briefly, I tucked a five into the greasy pocket of the bum's coat. I knew how he felt. The Santa Ana gets its name from the Mexican *satana*, or *devil wind*. It's a blinding, irritating dust storm that you can't ignore and you can't get away from and it doesn't let up for days. It's hell on the homeless. And I should know.

Because I'm one myself.

The bum began to snore. I moved away, headed back up Highland. The snores behind me diminished with distance. I smiled wryly. Like the bum behind me, I, too, live on the streets.

But unlike him, I don't sleep. Ever. I've got a rare biological quirk called *insomnolence*, and it's been keeping me awake – and alive – for nine years now.

9

My name's Alexander L'Hiboux. The last name's French, meaning the Owl. It's my real name – a poetic coincidence, nothing more. Comes from an Iroquois grandfather, as does my bone structure and the fact that I don't have to shave.

My grandfather also left me one other thing. I wear it in the shoulder holster under my left arm.

Technically, I guess you could call me a private detective. But I have no legal standing as such, since I have no license and make no arrests. But I've never left a case unsolved – and there have been a lot of cases.

Enough to fill a cemetary.

It's not exactly a good life on the streets of Los Angeles – even though I'm better off than most. I *do* have an unreal amount of money. However, I *don't* have a home. Nor a car. And for very good reason. You see, a home can be watched; a car can be bombed – and a lot of people want me dead. I stay alive because I can never be found. I never stop moving – and when I'm on a case, I never stop hunting.

Because I am the Owl. And the Owl never sleeps.

I do get hungry, though. So, about 3 p.m. or thereabouts, I paused to munch a greaseburger at Anthony's grill on Sunset. The burger wasn't bad, but the junkies that hung around the outside tables were a decided annoyance. If you looked at them they asked you for money, and I didn't feel like conversation. So I looked out at the sidewalk instead. And my stomach suddenly got cold.

A man stood there, looking at me. A man, not very tall, in work shirt and jeans. His hair and eyes were black, and his face was as dark and hard as hammered bronze. He looked at me, then across the street, toward Hollywood High. My eyes flicked to follow his gaze.

There was a blue Ford idling against the curb in the no-parking zone in front of the school. Unusual. I glanced back at the dark man.

He was gone. My stomach knotted further. Alcatraz was an enigma in my life, and not a pleasant one. Seeing him was a portent of incipient disaster, like the first hints of the brewing wind. I looked back at the car.

10

Three men were in it, hazy and indistinct in the wavering shimmers of heat rising from Sunset Boulevard. The sight made me feel hotter. I had already unzipped the sleeves from my jacket, but discarding the jacket itself might have excited comment.

Besides, the longer I gazed at the quietly rumbling car across the street, the stronger was my feeling that I would need the jacket – and very soon.

If I'd had any sense, I would've left right then. But I'd been short on sense for nine years now, and a well-developed nose for trouble has yet to keep me out of any. There was trouble in the air; an olfactory ozone-scented beacon of brewing disaster.

With a fatalistic grin, I checked my watch. 2:52.

I stood, stepping over a notably odorous and possibly dead gentleman lying in the shade of the Anthony's roof awning and entered the establishment next door. This billed itself as The Wine Cellar and catered to those whose discriminating palates preferred their wines with screw-off caps. The proprietor was a heavy-set Oriental who spoke only Spanish. Typical of the neighborhood.

After failed attempts in English, Japanese, Chinese and Korean, I finally got a reaction by swearing in frustrated Mexican slang and we were able to do business.

"Got any of those CO_2 bottle openers?" I asked.

He studied me carefully from behind a haze of cigarette smoke. "No, *señor*," he shrugged. "Don' sell them *chingazos* no more. Too dangerous."

"So I heard." I accidentally dropped a five on the counter and looked away, idly. "It's too bad, though . . . I'm a collector."

"I'll see." He didn't move, but when I had turned around, the five had vanished and a long white box had taken its place on the counter. Magic. The fat man shrugged again and blew more smoke.

"Forty dollar, *ese*."

Robbery at half the price. I paid without a murmur and picked up the oblong box. It was the general shape of a cheap coffin – an accidental bit of foreshadowing on the part of the manufacturer.

"*Gracias.*" I picked up the green cylinder that came with it and left the store.

The Pocket Rocket. A bad idea gone worse in the hands of the undesirable element. I dropped the CO_2 cartridge inside the hollow handle and screwed the cap back on. As I cocked the spring-loaded puncture mechanism, I remembered the short-lived legal life of such devices.

The "Li'l Corker". That was what the manufacturer called it. An effortless corkscrew. It had sounded good – in theory. What it amounted to was a hollow icepick with a compressed gas cartridge inside. You shoved the icepick needle through a winebottle's cork and filled the bottle with compressed gas, causing the cork to leap from the bottle with a bit of a bang. In practice, however, a number of flawed wine bottles had exploded like small bombs – but that was a minor problem. The major problem had been the almost simultaneous discovery of the device's extremely effective use as a weapon. Shoved almost anywhere into a human being, the quickly nicknamed "Pocket Rocket" instantly induced a massive pulmonary embolism that would drop a man as effectively as a magnum and as quietly as a knife.

A nasty weapon, with a vile history. It would do nicely. I dropped it in my pocket and headed up the street.

3:03. Two men emerged from the car and walked a short distance away from it. They were looking across the street, toward Anthony's and the liquor store. One was blond and sleek, the other darker, with a small moustache. Both were well-built, and conservatively, even tastefully, dressed. The blond one carried a manila envelope full of papers. He shook the envelope at the liquor store and said something inaudible. I leaned back against the dusty brick wall of a recording studio and pulled my baseball cap down low over my shades.

It would be nice to be wrong.

3:05 Across the street, the schoolbells rang for the day's release and about a billion kids vomited forth from every

12

pore of the dusty pink building. A mass of stylish sophisti-
cation and acne, the students reflected the area – products
of a fashion-conscious environment and concentrated adver-
tising campaigns.

One in particular caught my eye. A small, pretty female,
maybe sixteen, with a searing topknot of flame-colored hair
tied in odd places with gold lace ribbon.

Nothing unusual in that, of course. What *had* attracted my
attention were two things. One: she was walking alone. And
two: the pair of suits I had been observing had abandoned
all pretense of being legitimate real-estate speculators. They
were moving on her with serious purpose.

Sighing, I dropped a hand into my jacket pocket and
brought out the gleaming steel needle of the gas-powered
corkscrew. And even as I began running, I felt it: the first hot
breaths of a desert wind whistling down the Boulevard.

I don't know. Maybe I just *like* trouble.

Across the street, the roar of an engine mixed with the
startled shriek of a redheaded adolescent. I stepped off
the sidewalk, moving fast. The blue Ford tore away from
the curb in a hard left across the congested traffic of
Sunset, toward Lamont. The girl's legs still dangled from
the doorway, kicking in the air as startled horns blared. The
blond man was still outside, shoving for the door at a dead
sprint. He made it. So did I.

The car hit me head-on. My breath burst from my body
with an instantaneous *hufffff!* as I sprawled across the hood.
Slamming the windshield with my left shoulder, I brought my
right fist down in a hard, vicious arc. Six inches of stainless
steel needle punched through hood and air filter like so much
tinfoil. I heard a sharp, popping *hisss!* as the car swerved,
rolling me over the roof and dropping me to the hot, dirty
asphalt of Lamont. I hit with a slam I didn't feel and was
up again and moving fast even as thirty cubic centimeters
of ice-cold CO_2 blasted through the needle into the Ford's
carburetor.

The engine died without a sputter. Behind me, people
were only starting to react to the situation, shouting and

blowing their horns. I ignored them. Ahead of me, the Ford was coasting to a halt, the starter grinding ineffectually . . .

The last suit in was the first one out when I got there. Halfway out. That's when my shoulder caught him and slammed him back into the car doorway. Rebounding, I grabbed the door and threw it shut with my body weight behind it. Blondie's head was in the way. He dropped to the ground, bleeding copiously from the ears.

One down. I vaulted the trunk and met Moustache coming out the other side. My heels hit his gut hard enough to jar my fillings. He folded, retching, and I brought my elbow down on the base of his skull, just where it connects with the spine. Limbs twitching spasmodically, he thudded to the tarmac as I whirled. Somewhere, in the back of my mind, I was aware of the girl screaming. It made a weird, undulating resonance with the wind and the horns; a howling song of panic and heat.

The driver was out, his hand emerging from the inside of his suitcoat. Light shone dully from the Parkerized finish of his silenced ·22 automatic. Even as he shot me in the chest, I felt a great sense of relief. A silenced ·22 was a torpedo's weapon. The nagging fear that I'd been interfering with some law operation was stilled.

Now I could get rough.

His first shot was a staggering hammerblow to the chest. So was his second. He didn't get a third. A hot wind howled around the corner and blew open my bulletproof battle jacket, exposing for an instant the twin shoulder holsters that housed my own armament. And in that instant, my right hand yanked out cold blue iron.

Baroom! Baroom! Barroom! The Peacemaker roared in .45 *basso profundo* as my left palm slammed the hammer. The driver's body went three feet backward without touching the ground and hit asphalt in a heap. What was left of his head landed a good deal further on, as the last vestiges of crimson spray blew away on the dry and dusty wind. The Santa Ana tasted blood – and it howled.

In all, less than fifteen seconds had passed. Only now were people starting to cross the snarled traffic, shouting and gesticulating. Annoyances. Reaching inside the Ford, I got a firm grip and yanked. A squirming, redheaded mass emerged in my fist. I threw it away and thumbed the hammer.

Boom! The gas tank went up in a searing flame. Sufficient distraction. I turned and went away from there.

Fortunately, only one good citizen had the presence of mind to get in the way. I left him clutching a broken nose and pelted away down Morrow. Behind me were shouts, confusion, and running feet.

One of the pairs of running feet were coming after me.

I ducked into an alley beside a carwash and skidded to a halt, bringing my right fist across my chest. As the feet approached the corner, I started my swing.

The hard, bony corner of my elbow missed the crimson topknot by a half-inch and crunched into the brown brick of the building. I expressed myself in Spanish again.

The girl shook my arm, frantically.

"Please!" Her voice was melodious, not that it mattered at the moment. She shook my arm again. "Please, mister! Can you get me out of here, get me home?"

This is what comes of getting involved. The Owl is no white knight. I gave the girl a sour look as the whine of distant sirens began approaching.

"Getting out of here is just what I had in mind," I grumbled. "If you can keep up, come on."

She gave it a good try. Fortunately for her, the current vogue in women's footwear was a type of colorful sneaker. She'd never have kept the pace in heels.

We beat it down back alleys in a southeasterly direction until we hit Fountain, where I flagged a passing independent cab. He had no radio, so I figured we'd be safe for the moment.

"Sixth and Main, downtown," I said, choosing a direction at random. I wasn't picky, so long as it was far away. The

15

driver, a stolid Iranian type, nodded in wooden wordlessness. He pulled the cab in a smooth U-turn and headed east on Fountain.

The wind blew dust and red dirt against the glass with a soft, spattering noise. I looked away, at the sudden and unwanted companion I had so unfortunately acquired. She was still gulping in hysteria and gasping for breath, half-collapsed against the cheap vinyl seat. Obviously, she was in no condition for questioning, but the Owl is a less than kind person. It ruffles my feathers a tad when I have to shoot people without knowing why.

"What's your name, girl?"

"Huff." A slim brown hand with two gold bracelets at the wrist pushed a crimson tuft out of the jade-green eyes. The tan didn't sync with the hair color. Redhead's don't tan that well. No doubt a dye job.

"Scarlet," she panted. "Scarlet Serenade."

I'd had another question ready, but this made me forget what I was going to say. "You're kidding."

She was already flushed from running in the heat, but my response turned her a little pinker.

"Well, actually, it's Sarah Scarlotti, but I'm gonna change it." She sat up, suddenly, looking out the window of the cab. "Where are you taking me? I want to go *home*."

"Take it easy." The driver was looking at me in the rearview. Probably thought I was a white slaver. I gestured at him. "Give the man an address. I just wanted to get us moving."

"5707 Carol, North Hollywood." I looked at the driver and nodded. The silent one shrugged and turned left at the next intersection. The freeway was only a block or two ahead.

She was quiet as we mounted the ramp to the northbound 101 and merged with traffic. Her tan was growing paler, and the small hands were beginning to shake. Shock was setting in. When she began to gulp a little, I judged it was time to get her talking again. Last thing I needed was her blowing lunch all over me. Detracts from the heroic image.

"Who *were* those guys?" I wished the questions could be more specific, but the cabbie was listening. The girl shook her head, dully.

"I don't know." A lie, but not malicious. She was just trying not to think. The gulps started again, indicating a lack of success along those lines. She shuddered at a sudden recollection. "Who *are* you? A cop?"

I sighed. I was in deeper than I liked already. No point in getting any further involved. "No. You don't want to know."

"I can believe that," she muttered. Looking out the window, she drew away from me a little.

Through the chinks in the rattletrap cab, the gusting wind chuckled to itself, as though it knew a secret joke. We completed the rest of the journey in silence.

On my instructions, the cab let me off around the corner and a block from the girl's home. There was a decent possibility that the cops at the earlier fracas had established her indentity by now. In which case, they might send a squad car around to her address. I have an allergy to cops which is best handled by distance.

I gave the driver a C-note as I exited. Conscience money. The cops would eventually trace us to him. Once they did, he would probably spend the better part of a day answering questions.

"Mister?" The girl finally broke her long silence as I started to shut the door. The wind gusted, shoving at the door and ruffling the flame-red topknot. Green eyes looked up at me, unnaturally stark against the sickly pallor of her face. "Thanks . . . I guess."

"Yeah." I slammed the door against the wind. "No problem."

I have seldom made a wronger statement.

2

For some reason, I didn't walk away as quickly as I should have. The cab disappeared around the corner, and the wind pushed me along after it. I drifted up to the corner, where from the vantage point of a street marker I could see the cab. It stopped at a house four doors down.

Nice street. North Hollywood was mostly a dump, but it had some nice areas. This was one. An upper-class suburban neighborhood of expensively-watered lawns and trim green shrubbery. It was all turning a khaki color now in the windblown dust. As the girl got out of the cab, I noticed that every house in the neighbourhood was shuttered against the Santa Ana; windows closed and blinds drawn. The houses didn't look at me, and neither did the girl. Head bowed and steps slow, she shuffled to the house like a brightly colored little bird with tar in its feathers. I watched her crimson mop blowing around her downcast face as she unlocked the door. She stepped inside, and the wind blew red dust between us. I felt an odd sense of loss. I still had no idea what it had all been about.

Oh, well. I supposed I could read about it in the papers.

The wind shifted as I turned, came blowing from down the street. A sadistic spirit, it carried dust and blowing leaves, and a faint, muffled scream of terror, quickly shut off.

I gave a frustrated whimper and ran. I wasn't out of this yet.

When I got to the front door, I knocked politely with both feet and landed inside with the Peacemaker as my calling card. The big Colt noticed somebody with a gun turning in our direction and took him out of its own accord. That left one other contender, a pockmarked gentleman with a 9mm

18

Beretta in one hand and Sarah in the other. The sleek auto was pressed against the girl's right ear, and Pockmarks was shielding himself behind her. I showed him the inside of my smoking barrel, but the bastard was short and I couldn't get a clear shot around the girl. Besides, I only had one bullet left. I hadn't been able to reload in the taxi.

Pockmarks sneered. "Dramatic," he admitted, "but messy. You should work on your entrances."

He had a point. With the uncanny accuracy that instinctive snap shots so often have, I had plugged his partner neatly between the eyes. Some white lace drapes were now decorated with what had been inside his skull. However, his was not the only body in the room. Tied to a pair of expensive-looking black lacquer chairs were what was left of a middle-aged couple. They had been worked over with a number of instruments, some sharp, some blunt. I assumed they were Sarah's parents. A few hours ago, they had probably been a handsome couple. They weren't any more. It was a good thing I was keeping my eyes on Pockmarks, because I didn't want to look at them. The room stank of blood – with an odd petroleum overtone.

"You should talk," I said, indicating the mangled bodies. My gun didn't waver. Pockmarks frowned at me over the frantic girl's crimson pompadour.

"You're not a cop." It was a statement. "Who are you?"

"Al L'Hiboux." I spared a glance at Sarah. Though Pockmarks had his hand over her mouth, I could see that she was gulping queasily again. Her eyes were fixed on the mutilated bodies of her parents. She was so pale she looked green.

Pockmarks wasn't paying any attention. He had recognized the name.

"The Owl?" He looked faintly impressed. I have something of a reputation among society's dregs, being one of them myself. Pockmarks frowned again, as a thought struck him, and clutched the girl tighter. He began to edge slowly toward the door.

"But you're no bodyguard." It was an accusation, as though I'd been infringing on a union job. "This has nothing to do with you. Back off."

"Sorry." I kept the gun pointed at him, but he was adroitly keeping the girl in front. "I'm moonlighting today. So don't try to escape. Let the girl go."

He really sneered at that one. I didn't blame him. I sounded like a T.V. cop.

"No way, L'Hiboux. I need her." The girl struggled in his grip and he yanked her tighter against him, grinding the gun into her temple. Her eyes were bulging. "But that won't stop me from killing her if you try to shoot me." He began edging toward the door again.

"Oh, I'm *going* to shoot you,' I reassured him. It seemed a good idea to make that point clear. Idly, I noticed several gas cans scattered around the room. That explained the smell. Obviously, the two men had been planning on covering their tracks.

Sarah was gulping again, so I pressed the point. It wouldn't take much . . . "I'm gonna blow your head apart in a big messy spray of blood and brains . . . your eyeballs'll burst . . . "

He was staring at me in odd fascination, but it wasn't him I was talking to. The girl was white. She struggled desperately, and he tightened his grip absently, forcing her back against him. They were practically cheek to cheek, his hand over her mouth. I continued, in my best bedtime voice: " . . . And your body'll jerk all over the rug as your neck spurts blood . . . "

"*Hagurrrfff!!!*" Score! The little redhead vomited explosively, fountaining bile out of her nose and through his fingers. Because of his hand, it splashed all over his face and he reacted as any human being instinctively would under the circumstances.

"Yeccch!" he retched – and pushed her away.

Boom! Actually, I had given a pretty fair summation of what would happen when I pulled the trigger, but I had left out a couple of minor details. One was that a little teenage girl would be trying, with reasonable success, to heave her guts up in the corner of the room. The other was that as Pockmark's body convulsed in death throes on the rug, his gun would clench reflexively a few times. One of the bullets went through a gas can and the next thing I knew, we were in Hell.

I staggered back as the flames roared up in a searing wall, feeling my hair singe just from proximity. Fortunately, the fire was not between me and the door. It was the matter of an instant for me to search Pockmark's pockets, after which I beat a hasty retreat. As the house smoke alarms started buzzing frantically, I dragged a still-retching teenager out of the door and back into the howling wind.

There was a white Camaro parked outside. I had barely noticed it before, but it sure looked good to me now. Pockmark's keys fit it. Tossing the redhead inside, I jumped in myself and had the thing moving even before the Santa Ana blew the door shut. From the corner of my eye, I could see the hot glare of the fire burning through the house's windows. Only seconds before it would be breaking through the outer structure and be noticed. I got out of there.

Sarah was slumped in her seat, staring in mute melancholy at her fingernails. She had vomit on her clothes, and her flaming red hair was in disarray. Silent tears were running down her motionless face, as though they were being poured. She wasn't making any noise at all.

The interior of the car was beginning to reek of puke. I rolled down the window. She was in no condition for questioning. But by this time I was in no mood for waiting. I spoke.

"Were those your parents in the—"

Scream! A wordless howl, it ripped explosively from her tiny body. My ears rang with it. Dimly, I heard the wind outside answer it as she began to sob – hard, uncontrollable sobs; the kind that hurt. Rocking with each spasm, choking, little fists clenched against her chest and tears streaming, she was slamming her crimson topknot against the padded dash with each convulsion. The wind gusted, rocking the car from side to side. The hell with it. I couldn't drive while all this was going on. I pulled into an alleyway and stopped the car.

"Hey, calm down." I come up with great lines like that sometimes. She paid no attention, of course, whooping and sobbing and rocking and retching. Hysterical, she was starting to hyperventilate. In the movies, the macho guy always solves this with a stiff smack across the face. But in certain circumstances, even the Owl shows mercy. The girl had been through enough.

There was a plastic litter bag hanging from the air-conditioner knob in the car. I pulled it off, constricted the opening with my right hand, and blew into the bag, inflating it. Then I grabbed a handful of red hair in my left fist and shoved the bag over her nose and mouth. Green eyes looked up at me, startled. Her hands, strong with the andrenal rush of panic, struggled to push me away, but I held tight. Her gasping breaths inflated, deflated, inflated the bag again. Gradually, she began to calm as the carbon-dioxide buildup in her blood made her drowsy. The spasming stopped, and she stopped shoving at me. Slowly, I took the bag away from her mouth and put it in her hands.

"Just sit for a while," I said. "If you feel yourself getting out of control again, start breathing into the bag."

She nodded, saying nothing, and I settled back into the driver's seat, starting the car again. We had to get further away from the house.

I drove the Camero out of the alley and back onto a main street. Beside me, the girl was breathing into the bag. Moving fast, but going nowhere. It was how I felt about the whole situation.

Outside, the red wind rocked the car and chuckled.

3

It was getting close to 5 p.m. Four, maybe five guys dead in less than two hours. Not bad, I've done better, but hey, it was a Monday. Maybe once I found out what the hell was going on, I could get my average up. I snarled slightly, but permitted the silence to last until I had steered the Camaro up the 101 southbound onramp and merged with the thick traffic.

"Okay, now." I steered with one knee as I pulled out the Peacemaker and started jacking out spent shells. It goes against the Owl's paranoid nature to holster an empty gun. "Start talking. What's going on?"

The girl's eyes were widening at the sight of fat ·45 rounds sliding into the cylinder with ominous clicks. A calculated move, I do admit. But it did loosen her tongue at last.

"Uh, I'm not real sure . . . "

"Crap."

"But I don't *know*!"

I holstered the Colt with an audible thump. It made her jump slightly. I smiled a sweet, gentle smile from behind the shades. I doubt if it was reassurring. I didn't mean it to be.

"Little lady," I said, with extraordinary patience, "I have been scattering bodies all over Los Angeles County because of you. You may not know me. You may not like me. But at the moment it looks like I'm the best friend you've got. So I ask again. What's going on?"

She bit her lip and looked out the window at a tumbleweed, being blown along the freeway at almost the same speed as the traffic. "I can't tell you."

The steering wheel cracked in my grip, but I maintained a cool demeanor.

"Fine. Then I drop you off at a cop station and say goodbye."

"No!"

"Hum."

"What?"

"So it's that kind of trouble, eh?"

She turned back, glowering defensively. "Maybe . . . sorta . . . well, what do *you* care?"

"I'm a good citizen."

"That man called you the Owl."

"I'm a good citizen."

"*Are* you the Owl?"

I kept my eyes on the road. The tumbleweed was still ahead of us, bouncing along merrily in the left lane. Cars swerved to avoid it. "I believe *my* question was first. What's going on?"

She looked out at the tumbleweed. A last merry bounce, then the Santa Ana had a cruel streak and threw it under a truck. Instant splinters. They blew away in the swirl of wind and traffic and were gone. The sight seemed to take some of the starch out of the girl.

"I guess it's Jason." The voice was low, almost inaudible.

"Boyfriend?"

"Sorta."

"Sorta?"

"Well, kinda."

I ground a tooth or two and decided that there must be a knack to interrogating teenage girls. I shifted the question.

"What's he done?"

"Nothing. Are you the Owl?"

"No. What's he done? Why are people after you?"

"Yes you are."

Extremely patient, with teeth clenched: "What — has — he — done? Why — are — people — after — you? Why — were — your — *parents killed*!?"

Oops. Losing the cool ever so slightly there. I should have just slapped her. Would have been kinder.

"*Ooomp-ooomp-ooomp* . . . "

"Use the bag."

She began to wail and gulp at the same time, a dangerous combination. I picked up the litter bag and held it out to her.

"Use the bag!"

She threw up all over my arm.

I sighed and rolled the window down further. This was a great job.

Losing her lunch did seem to calm her a bit, though. She settled back, gulping in scared embarrassment, while I daubed at my arm with an ineffectual handkerchief. Fortunately, she'd already dumped most of her lunch back at her house. I threw the handkerchief into the back seat.

"Sorry," she said.

"So'm I," I grumbled. "This brave defender shit is beginning to lose a bit of its glamor."

"I'm sorry."

"Stop being sorry. Talk."

She pulled a tuft of hair around and began gnawing on it. "Well, it's . . . like . . . I don't know. It's hard to know where to start . . . "

"Jason."

"Yeah . . . "

"He's your boyfriend. And he's done something. And now people are trying to kidnap you."

"Well, he's not my boyfriend . . . "

"Excuse me. I should have said 'sorta'."

"He's Allegra's boyfriend. She's my best friend."

I digested this a moment in silence. "Um. But you think he might be more interested in you."

She colored. "Well, yeah. Sorta."

"And you sorta have a reason to sorta think so."

She got pinker. "Yeah."

I didn't press the point. "Do you think that this . . . Allegra? . . . is behind the assaults?"

She gave me a scornful look. "No way! She's my friend! Besides, like, she's only sixteen, same as me."

Well, that didn't make it impossible, but it *was* less likely. I went back to the first track.

"Okay . . . now, this Jason – what's his last name?"

"Um . . . Magrina."

"Is Jason Magrina sixteen too?"

"No . . . he's twenty-one, I think."

"You're not sure?"

"No. He's something like that."

This was more promising. "Is he a student? College or something?"

"No . . . "

"So, what's he do?"

"Well, he . . . sold stuff . . . "

"Drugs." Suddenly, it was all becoming very clear.

"Not like *that* . . . " she protested. "I mean, it's not like he's a *pusher* or anything. It's just, like, guys wanted it, y'know, and he got it for them. Y'know?"

"Sure." A dealer. In all my years walking the streets of Los Angeles, I had yet to meet a single "pusher". There was no need for anyone to "push" drug use. The media and simple human curiosity did that. The drugs did the rest. No dealer actively solicited for new clients – most dealers were hard-pressed to supply the customers they already had. But more kept coming. They always would.

I was losing interest. Although I have an ingrained dislike for drug dealers, the rightness or wrongness of drug use was no concern of mine. I don't deal in felonies. There are laws and cops enough for those. The Owl dispenses specialized justice for people who have no other option – and nowhere else to turn. And this didn't look like my kind of game.

I cleared my throat. "I don't like dealers. I only got involved because I thought you needed my help. Now you're safe, so I figure I'm about through. You got a relative or somebody I can take you to?"

She was looking hurt. Possibly because my voice was cold, but more likely because I had reminded her she was now an orphan.

"No." The melodious voice was small and timid.

"Brothers? Sisters? Grandparents?"

" . . . No . . . " Weaker now. "Just my . . . *parents* . . . !" She started wailing again.

"Aw, *man* . . . " I was really out of my element in this kind of situation. Awkwardly, I reached over and patted her shoulder. She immediately slid over and started crying on my Kevlar. Having no place else to put my arm, I draped it over her shoulder. It might have looked romantic, but she was in emotional pain and only half my age. Besides, we both smelled of barf.

"Look, I'm sorry," I continued, a bit lamely. "How about friends? You could maybe use some emotional support . . . "

Sniffling, she shook her head against the battle jacket. The shoulder holster beneath ground into my ribcage. "No . . . I gotta find Jason!"

Man, this guy must be a real ladykiller. "Don't you think he's caused you enough trouble?"

"But it *wasn't* him!" she protested wetly. "It wasn't his fault . . . I wanted him to stop dealing, and he said he would . . . but then he got ripped off!"

"Huh?" A keen, insightful question.

"Yeah . . . see, he had this last stash – it wasn't his, he was holding it – and it got ripped off! Now the guys he was holding it for want it back, and they think he faked the rip-off, but he didn't. But he was scared they were going to mess him up, so he took off to look for the guys who ripped him off, y'know?" She had straightened, and was pulling on my jacket earnestly. I pushed her gently back over to the passenger side. I don't like anyone that close to my guns.

"So who's after you?"

She shook her head. "I dunno. Maybe the guys who ripped him off, 'cause he's coming after them?" This was spoken hopefully.

I frowned. "More likely, the guys who owned the shit. They want his head, and they figure you can lead them to him."

"Maybe." Sour. The possibility had occurred to her, too, but the other hypothesis made the boyfriend look better. Chicks are weird.

27

"What was the stuff, anyway?"

"Coke."

"How much was there?"

"Um . . . Six pounds, I think . . . I'm not sure."

I raised an eyebrow, did a little quick figuring. Six pounds of cocaine . . . figure it gets stepped on a couple times . . . oh, say, a quarter of a million bucks. No showstopper these days, but enough to get a few people killed. It explained the rough treatment of her parents, anyway. No doubt they had been interrogated on the whereabouts of their daughter's boyfriend.

"Six pounds." I grumbled, steering the Camaro around a slow-moving red Bug. "Not much in the overall market, but it's a lot more than most dealers have on hand. Your boyfriend was moving up into the big leagues."

"It wasn't his! He was holding it for somebody!"

"Yeah. Well, my advice is stay out of it. Don't try to find him. You can't do him any good, and you might easily get killed yourself."

"I can help him."

"Oh, right."

"I *can*!"

"How?" I asked, not unreasonably. "So far, you've been about as helpful as a shooting gallery duck."

"I . . . know something. Something that will help him."

"And that is?"

She looked sad and stubborn. "I can't tell you. I can only tell Jason."

Jesus. It sounded right out of a soap opera. I snorted derisively. "You're pregnant."

It was a joke, of course. But when she gave me that wild-eyed look and then touched her belt timidly, as though checking to see if she was showing, I felt sick inside.

"You are?" My voice lacked the usual macho timbre. I cleared my throat as she nodded, sombrely.

"I didn't think it showed. I'm not far along."

"Lucky guess." I stared out the windshield, watching the truck ahead sway in the wind gusts. As we drew abreast

28

I switched lanes, moving further left. Trucks can be dangerous during the Santa Ana. Not that I would normally have cared . . .

I cleared my throat again. "I'll . . . (ahem) I'll admit that the information does have a certain surprise quotient. But how in the . . . how on *earth* do you expect it to help him?"

She looked stubborn. "It will."

"How?"

She looked out the window. The 101 was headed due south at the moment, and because of the hills the Santa Ana was howling directly from the rear. The red Bug we had passed earlier came barrelling by us, propelled by the wind. The bulky driver at the wheel looked scared shitless. Bugs take on strange aerodynamic qualities in a Santa Ana. Sarah watched, without seeing.

"I want him to turn himself in. He didn't do much – he didn't hurt anyone, anyway. If he turns himself in, he'll be protected from those creeps, and the police and judges and stuff will be nicer to him. He'll probably just be put in one of those honor farms for a while, like where they put the Watergate guys." She touched her belt again.

"I . . . *we*'ll be waiting when he comes out."

I almost wanted to cry. The Owl is used to the rough and rugged practicality of the streets. Raw sentimental stupidity like this was a rare item. I didn't know whether to laugh, cry, or beat her over the head with a baseball bat.

Lacking the bat, and rejecting tears as unsuitably unmacho, I chose to laugh instead. This made her cry. This made me feel like a piece of shit.

"*Ooomp . . . ooomp . . . ooomp . . .*"

"C'mon, I'm sorry," I said, clumsily attempting to steer and pat her shoulder at the same time.

"I just want to *find* him!"

"I know, I know . . . but don't you think you'd be better off at some friend's house? Allegra, for instance?"

"Yeah, and have them end up like my *parents*?" She began crying on my jacket again.

It was a good point, I had to admit. "Well . . . what do you want from *me*?" I asked, knowing even as I said it that I was headed for trouble.

"Help me. Help me find Jason." The little redheaded moppet rubbed her nose on my jacket. What the hell, she'd dumped just about everything else there. "That's all . . . just help me find Jason. I can handle the rest."

Yeah, sure. "You don't know what you're asking. That's dangerous as hell."

"But . . . (sniffle) . . . you're – the *Owl*!"

And I ain't stupid. You're being dropped off at the next police station, and that's final! I didn't say. I meant to say it. I started to say it. But somehow, the words came out all jumbled.

"Yeah. Yeah, okay. Let's do it," I heard my voice saying. Dumb asshole.

Despite the wind, I kept the window down all the way to East Los Angeles. The ride hadn't improved the smell of either of us much. Exiting the freeway at Seventh Street, I turned left, away from the bridge. On the other side, the city lights were just beginning to glimmer against the setting sun. The sky was as red as Sarah's dye job. The Santa Ana makes for spectacular sunsets. Framed against it, even the ragged towers of Los Angeles looked beautiful – from a distance. We headed the other way.

This side of the L.A. River was the *barrio*. East L.A. It had a few other names. Boyle Heights was what the maps said. Nobody who lived there called it that.

It would do fine.

The car had been handy, but I had to get rid of it. There was a slight chance that someone in Sarah's neighborhood might have noted it. More importantly, it belonged to a guy who was now a hunk of roasted meat in the charred remains of Sarah's living room. Not that *he* would come looking for it. But he had been working for someone – and that someone was obviously a person or organization with a good deal of manpower. I had already stepped on their toes twice today. They would be looking for the car – and whoever was in it – with considerable vengeance in mind.

There are those amongst the criminal class, who, when faced with the job of car disposal, choose flamboyant methods. But shoving a car over a cliff into the ocean is not the Owl's style. Lacks finesse and, besides, that's littering. The Owl is a good citizen. I simply took the Camaro to the corner of Whittier and Soto and parked. We were just down the street from a white-iron taco stand, its parking lot filled with Hispanic subversives.

"Out," I said to the girl, who was leaning back against the seat, her hand over her eyes. She took the hand away and blinked at me.

"Where are we?"

"End of the line. Out." Suiting action to words, I opened the door. The wind swirled a potato-chip bag into the back seat. No matter. I popped the trunk release and the hood release next to the driver's seat and got out, shutting the door behind me.

The passenger door opened, grating slightly on the high concrete curb. Sarah's crimson head emerged, squinting into the wind.

"You forgot the keys."

"No, I didn't."

The trunk was bare, just a spare tire under the rug and a tire jack. About what I expected. I had already searched the glove compartment and dashboard during the drive down. Nothing. It would figure, though. They were all places a cop might check during a routine traffic stop.

Ah, but the hood. I lifted the lid and looked at an arsenal. A turbocharged, fuel-injected V8 engine takes up a lot of room in an engine compartment, but by no means all. A fiberglass-stocked, Leopould-scoped stainless-steel Sturm/Ruger M77 ·308 sniper rifle was clamped to one side, and an Ingram Mac-10 assault pistol on the other. The Ingram didn't take up much room, so a ·357 Taurus snubbie was strapped beside it. All were wrapped in polyethylene sheet to protect them from engine dirt.

"Hm," I said.

Sarah looked in. "Are those guns?"

"Brilliant. Hold on a second."

I went back to the trunk and reached up my left sleeve. Elvira emerged, four inches of vanadium steel blade glimmering in the twilight. I sliced away the gray rug covering the interior of the trunk in a ragged square and took it back with me to the engine compartment.

"What are you doing?" Inquisitive chick.

"A little disarmament." I pulled the weapons free of the clamps. Fortunately, the open hood was between me and the nearby parking lot, preventing anyone there from seeing what I was doing. As far as they knew, I was simply working on the engine. I dropped the pistol, assault carbine and sniper rifle into the rug, rolling them up into a heavy, rather awkward bundle. "No point in letting them fall into the wrong hands, where they might in the future be used against someone I care about very deeply."

"You?"

I glowered. "That was *my* punch line."

She smiled for the first time since I'd met her.

The wind blew the hood shut as I shoved the trunk lid closed. The car doors were locked, but the keys still dangled from the ignition. Fine. With the bundle under my left arm and the girl walking to my right, we strolled away down Whittier in the purplish twilight. The wind swirled dust and debris around our ankles with a scurrying, rustling noise, and Sarah unconsciously moved closer to me. An upscale Val was 'way off her turf in East L.A., and she knew it.

Nervously, she glanced back, the way we had come – and gasped.

"The car's gone!"

"I know," I said comfortably, although I had heard nothing. "Magic, huh?"

Turning the corner at Boyle, we walked on, into the wind.

A block down Boyle was Hollenbeck Park, one of L.A.'s least-known and most surreal public recreational facilities. A perfectly nice, normal, respectable park – except they had built the Santa Ana Freeway right over the top of it. Now trees, grass and lake were roofed over with a slab of concrete eight lanes wide and forty feet in the air. In the grotto thus formed beneath, the turgid lake supported a multitude of chubby ducks, an occasional grimy swan, and a mixed handful of drug dealers.

None of the latter were there at the moment, however. High winds are not conducive to crack sampling. For better or worse, we had the place to ourselves.

We walked down the slight hill, over the grass, and into the park itself. The dark, massive bulk of the freeway closed over us ominously – and loudly. The roar of the traffic on the Santa Ana freeway above mixed with the ungodly howl of the Santa Ana wind blowing amidst the concrete pillars below. The Santa Ana stereo. It sounded like someone had opened the gates of Hell.

There was a single light – an old-fashioned frosted Victorian spire set high atop a metal pillar. Unfortunate. I had counted upon its being broken. By all rights it should have been. City Maintenance must have replaced it recently. Like today. Oh, well. I shifted the load to my right hand, hauled out the Waster with my left, and fired. *Spak!* The poisoned Silver Jet pellet smashed the bulb with little fuss and almost no noise. Darkness closed in. Only the distant lights of the run-down apartments surrounding the park reflected in the wind-chopped lake water. In the blackness, I could sense the girl looking at me quizzically.

"A BB gun?"

"Sorta." I replaced the Philippine assassin's weapon in the right-hand shoulder holster and hefted the bundle again. "Hang on a second."

The rug-wrapped bundle hit the dark lake water with an oily splash and sank out of sight. With any luck it would stay there – at least until the guns within were too corroded to be used again. I watched until the bubbles had stopped rising and the ducks had stopped quacking in alarm, then turned back to the girl.

"Good enough. Let's go."

The dim outline of the girl shivered in the warm wind. She wasn't cold, just tired and scared. It had been a rough

33

day. "Where?"

"First, away from here." I turned my back on the lake walking toward the embankment that lead up to the roadway I had barely gotten past the dumpsters when the shadowy form jumped out at me.

" 'ey, *homeboy* . . . "

I sank a right in his gut and a left to his jaw. As he reeled sideways, I kicked him hard, in the chest. He flipped backward and landed hard, flat on his back and gasping for breath I cocked the Peacemaker in his face and was reaching for the pencil flash before Sarah's scream had even finished echoing around the concrete pillars.

"Move and die, asshole," I gritted at him over the blue steel barrel. The pencil flash clicked on.

"Uhhh . . . " Tears ran from his eyes and down his grizzled cheeks. Sarah had been drawing breath to scream again but paused, stepping forward instead. Together, we looked down upon a scrawny Mexican, wearing a grimy coat, no shirt, tattered pants and no shoes. He whimpered in terror, holding his chest painfully and rolling his eyes at the cocked ·45.

"*No . . . no . . . no . . .* "

Sarah's voice sounded sadly in my ear.

"I think he just wanted a handout, Owl."

"Yeah." I holstered the Peacemaker ashamedly. Jitters or not, I had to be more careful. Sarah was helping the old guy back to a sitting position.

"*Está bien? Muy apologiso, amigo.*" I was mildly surprised. Her Spanish was better than mine – not that that was saying much. I mostly just know the swear words. I guess the kids learn something at school after all. Peeling a C-note from my wad, I bent and extended it to him, the green fluttering in the wind. Eyes flashing at me angrily, Sarah snatched it away.

"Don't try to buy him off – he's a human, he has his dignity—"

"*No! Aqui!*" The old guy snatched the bill back from her and hugged it to his chest. That bill would buy a lot of wine.

Maybe even some food. Sarah looked surprised, then looked up at me. I shrugged, and helped her back to her feet.

Some things you just have to learn on the street.

As we trudged away up the embankment, we could hear the old guy singing wheezily in the dark, accompanied by the quavering whistle of the wind. The traffic noise grew louder as we got higher. Panting a little, the girl came up beside me.

"You don't have to kill *everybody*, you know, Owl."

"Don't call me Owl.

It had been a hell of a Monday.

TUESDAY

4

The sun rose like a copper ball over the low roofs of East L.A., the red winds swirling around it like a Sahara dust storm. Six a.m. and it was already eighty degrees. The dust prickled on the back of my neck.

We'd made it as far as the railroad yard near the L.A. River before Sarah had collapsed. A long and traumatic day on a very empty stomach had taken their toll. Now she was curled up in one of the empty boxcars while I sat impatiently on guard. Six hours is a long time for the Owl to stay in one place. Being saddled with a person who sleeps is almost as bad as having to sleep myself.

In the morning heat, the boxcar smelled of old manure and oil. The wind whistled through the slats of the half-opened doorway and blew Sarah's short shirt up over her left hip. She stirred a little, her slender legs stretching in the warm dimness of the car.

They were nice legs. Young, slim, tanned and nice. I felt a stirring in my groin which for some reason only made me feel old and tired. So I got to my feet and headed for the downwind door. Figured I'd go take a leak.

"Hey! What's going on here?"

Damn the wind. The muttering howl had masked his steps and I hadn't heard him coming. A burly man with a misshapen nose and grimy coveralls, he stepped up to the doorway and glowered at me.

"Get out."

Since the height of the boxcar floor gave me a four-foot advantage, I stayed where I was. "Who are you?"

39

"Yard supervisor. Now get out of there." He was holding a three-foot prybar in one solid fist and he hefted it meaningfully. "Or I come in."

Either way meant a fight, and I wasn't in the mood. I hardened my face behind the wrap around shades.

"Just back off, buddy. Everything's cool. We'll be gone in a few minutes."

"We?" In the dimness, he hadn't noticed the girl. Swivelling his head around, he looked toward the far end of the boxcar. Sarah sat up dazedly, moaning and rubbing her eyes. And the man in front of me exploded.

"You sonofaBITCH!" He shoved the hooked end of the prybar forward, snagging me around the left ankle just as I was jumping back. My Peacemaker cleared leather, but his furious yank on the prybar sent me crashing to the boxcar's plywood floor. BOOM! The big ·45 went off as I hit, the slug tearing a gaping hole in the roof. Wood splinters and manure dust rained down, blowing and swirling in the hot wind. Sarah screamed.

The bastard was fast. A sweep of the prybar sent my pistol clattering across the floor, and as I rolled after it, he came sailing through the door to land on my back. The prybar crashed down on my head. I saw stars.

Fortunately, my baseball cap is reenforced with fiberglass or I'd have been looking at a concussion. As it was, I merely rolled to a crouch, shaking my head to clear it. And the first thing I saw was the inside of the Peacemaker's muzzle.

The flintlike eyes glared at me over the still-smoking barrel of my own gun. "Don't move, you bastard."

His finger was on the trigger, but he hadn't cocked the hammer. Single-action revolvers are tricky if you aren't used to them. I figured I had a two-second lead, and one was all I would need. As the wind howled, my right hand slid toward my left wrist . . .

His eyes were red-rimmed pools of hatred. "I got me a daughter just her age, you filthy bastard," he spat. And his eyes softened in concern as he looked toward the still-gaping Sarah. "You all right, little honey?"

My stomach sank, and I took my fingers off the knife in my wrist-sheath. In the Owl's profession, the greatest danger is not the criminal, but the good citizen. They have an annoying habit of getting in my way, and killing them is not an option.

"It's not what you think. Sarah—"

"Shut up." He kept the gun pointed at me, but his concern was for the girl. "If you can walk, Miss, we'll head back to the yard office. This scum's got a date with the cops."

"I can walk." To my surprise, her voice was hushed and broken. I glanced over.

Sarah's eyes were red and teary as she got unsteadily to her feet. She moved with an air of humiliation and pain, whimpering as she huddled herself within her arms. Everything about her screamed that she'd been raped – and raped brutally. My jaw dropped.

The yard boss looked back at me with eyes as angry as the skies outside. "You diseased son of a bitch," he whispered – and raised the pistol to my face.

In the next instant he was staggering across the plywood floor as Sarah landed on his back. "Get him, Owl!" she shrieked.

Christ, spare me these amateurs. I'd already wrenched the pistol from his grasp. I stood there with it dangling from my fingers and watched. The burly man with the redheaded wildcat on his back collided with the grimy slats of the box-car wall, then lurched back in my direction. As they passed, I thumped the man's skull leisurely with the Peacemaker's butt: He dropped to the floor and stayed there.

Sarah rolled off him, panting and angry. She pushed flaming hair from her eyes and glared up at me.

"Jesus – take your time, why don't you? He could have killed me!"

I was already using the belt of the unconscious man's coveralls to lash his hands behind his back. A fairly pointless move, but I figured the poor guy deserved a few exciting embellishments to his story. He was going to have quite a headache.

"He's not the type," I said, and stood. Then I grabbed her by the topknot and lifted her to her tiptoes. She gasped in pain.

"But *I* am," I continued. My teeth were clenched in a dangerous grimace that was a long way from a smile. "So *I'll* handle the fighting, understand? The last thing I need is help from you."

"Yeah?" She yanked herself away, mouth twisting into an angry pout. "He was about to blow your head off!"

"Only because he thought I'd *raped* you – what the *hell* were you trying to pull, anyway!?"

"I was trying to *distract* him! *You* weren't doing shit!"

"The situation was under control. A couple words from you and he'd have calmed down. He was just trying to *rescue* you, for crissake. You want me to kill him for that?"

She subsided, blowing out a puff of air and looking at the man on the ground. Her voice was suddenly very small.

"No," she said. "No. I've seen enough . . . enough of that." She nodded at the body on the floor. "Is he all right?"

"Fortunately." I took her by the elbow and led her toward the downwind door. "But we've got to get out of here. The sooner I get you off my hands, the better I'll like it."

Landing on the gravel below, I turned and held up my hands. She jumped into my arms and clung there a moment. "I'm sorry I made you mad."

She was warm and light and soft. The wind tousled her hair and caressed my cheek with it. I quickly put her down on the ground.

"You sleep too much," I growled.

We walked off across the yard, toward the hills of Echo Park. The wind pattered gravel against our backs, the rattle and moan reminding me of dry bones.

Unbidden, a voice in my head finished the sentence. "*And you're too damn good a liar.*"

5

Elysian Park to Sunset, and I was starting to get nervous. There was a newspaper vending machine every damn block, and we'd made the *Times* headline. "HOLLYWOOD HIGH STUDENT ABDUCTED DURING GUN BATTLE" blared forth on twenty-point type everywhere I looked. I should have expected it. The *Times* staff always takes a perverse pride in the Owl's activities – because I used to work freelance for them. But that was a long, dark decade ago; before Alexander L'Hiboux, reporter, was reborn in a Hell of fire and rage as the ever-deadly, never-sleeping Owl.

"Oh, gross me," Sarah grumbled, after I bought a paper. The headline was accompanied by a year-old school photo of her, in which her hair was both shorter and darker. She eyed it with distaste. "Why'd they use *that* thing? I had head shots taken last month to send out. A stack this big."

"Were they at home?"

"Yeah – oh." Remembering the conflagration left behind. Twisting her mouth, she craned her neck to study the photo again.

There was a list of her vital statistics alongside, to help with public identification. I scanned them quickly. Height, weight, hair and eye color, date of birth, etc. They all seemed more or less accurate unfortunately. The date of birth seemed familiar for some reason. Probably because the day and month were the same as my own. The year was different, though. Very different. I shook my head and quickly turned to the article.

The by-line was by Kerry McCoy, a man who had been a friend ten years ago. Apparently he still was. He'd managed to garble my description nicely. But the warnings

43

were there: " . . . police have strong leads"; " . . . initial abductors were slain by a possible vigilante . . . " That sort of thing. They knew who it was, all right. The Owl's methods are as clear as a signature.

The wind gusted, folding the paper over in my face, but I'd read enough. The fact that Sarah had gone after me of her own volition had apparently escaped the witnesses' notice. I was now being sought as a kidnapper, along with the usual murder charges. The cops are usually pretty lackadaisical about tracking me down. They don't like criminal scum any better than I do. But this was different. So far, the only bodies that had been identified were Sarah's parents. And Sarah herself was missing. The cops weren't going to let this one slide. There was a manhunt brewing. I could feel it building, the way I could feel the Santa Ana's strength building in the distant desert. I was in for some serious hell.

Wadding the newspaper, I tossed it toward a public trashcan nearby. But the wind caught it, sweeping the ball off course and scattering a dancing flurry of papers wildly across the street. My intentions had been good, but the results were an unforeseen mess. Kind of like the past twenty-four hours.

"What?" She didn't like the sour look I was directing at her. "*Now* what're you pissed off about?"

"The whole damn city now thinks I kidnapped you," I grumbled. "And that performance you put on back at the railroad is *not* going to help things."

"Well, I *said* I was sorry."

"Don't talk to me, talk to the cops."

"I *will*, I swear! But I *have* to do it with Jason. He's the whole reason this is all happening. And if I can't save him . . . then everybody – my parents . . . " – she gulped – " . . . it will all have been for nothing."

I glowered at her as she wiped her nose quickly and continued, turning those big green eyes on me hopefully.

"It won't be much longer – really! Jason was renting this little house in Silverlake – it's not far—"

"Oh, come off it. After all this, no way he'd be there."

"He might. He got it as a hideout. It's not his real apartment—"

"He'd still be gone. If you know about it, then other people do. Too dangerous to stay."

"But there'd be *clues*, right? And you're a detective. You'll be able to figure out where he went."

Wonderful, this T.V. generation. Still, I'd come this far. It was worth a try.

"All right. But we do it my way." I frowned at her bright pink-and-gold outfit. "First off – you need to tone down a little. Got every cop in L.A. looking for us, and you're walking around like a neon sign." I indicated a thrift store just up the street. "Let's go shopping."

Kidnapping, gun battles, her parents murdered and the night spent in a boxcar, she was still a teenage girl. She bipped off into the store, radiating delight, and I dropped a quarter into the public phone outside. It was time to touch base with sanity.

Danny answered the phone on the first ring. "Investigations." An innocuous statement. I had no trouble remembering the passcode – the headlines were still burning in my memory.

"Hollywood," I said. The first word of the headline. By procedure Danny should have responded with the last. However, she seemed inclined to waive identification formalities at the moment.

"You goddamn insane sonofabitch!" came the furious response. "What the *hell* have you been doing?"

"Just being a good citizen—"

"You kidnapped a sixteen-year-old *girl*?"

"More the other way around, really."

"What?"

"She was *being* kidnapped. I interfered. Then I left, but she followed me. So I tried to take her home, but she ran into some more unpleasant types, who had already killed her parents. I managed to get her out alive, but it wasn't easy and the house burned down. Now she—"

45

I broke off. Through the window of the store, Sarah was beaming at me proudly, indicating the clothes she was now wearing. I gaped. Levis, a tan jacket, sunglasses, and hair tucked up under a baseball cap – she was a feminine replica of myself. "Ta-daaah!" Her voice came faintly through the shop window. "Twinsies!"

I frowned and shook my head sternly. She pouted behind the sunglasses, but turned back to the clothes rack.

"Yeah, I'm still here." Danny had been making noises in my ear. "But not for long. She wants to find her boyfriend – some kind of low-level dealer – and convince him to turn himself in to the cops. Apparently, he ripped off some hardball types, and what you read in the papers is the result. Me, I'm just an innocent bystander."

"Right." Danny's voice was as dry as the windblown dust.

"Hey, you know me."

"Yes, I do, Al. You're the Owl. You're an ice-blooded, two-fisted, merciless sonofabitch. You move fast, shoot faster, and never take unnecessary chances. You've stayed alive because you stay alone and out of sight. Yet now, all of a sudden, you've got the cops, the drug underworld, and probably the FBI on your ass – all because some sixteen year old *bimbo*—"

Oh, Christ, I thought. *I should have seen it coming.*

"—just *asked* you to!? Jesus, Al, have you gone senile? Or . . . " (suspiciously) " . . . does she have big tits?"

I grinned for the first time that day. "Watermelons," I confirmed, glancing in through the store window at Sarah's elfin frame. She'd changed the Owl outfit for dark jeans, an oversized blouse worn loose and a faded vest. She'd also strapped the hair back in a ponytail. Overall, the effect was agreeably mediocre. Just the way a low-profile type like the Owl prefers it. I gave her a thumbs-up through the window.

"That's what I thought." Danny knew bull when she heard it, but she was woman enough to be peeved anyway. "Well, I hope you're having fun, because you're paying quite a price for it. I've already received a couple of warning calls. People are asking around for you – and they're not all cops."

46

I frowned. That was bad. Though Danny's technical expertise had managed to bury the office phone number so deep that it wasn't even listed as "unlisted", it was known by any number of trusted bartenders around town. It was a fairly good system – people in need of the Owl's services were both desperate and despairing. Such types invariably ended up in bars. And bartenders hear enough sob stories to know a real Owl client when one turns up.

Still, it meant that an uncomfortable quantity of people knew the Owl's office number. And sooner or later it could lead to trouble.

"Better start setting up a backup number," I advised.

"Already did," said Danny smugly, reading it off. I committed it gratefully to memory. Being cut off from Danny would be like losing my ears. Her equipment and skills were part of what kept the Owl one jump ahead of the opposition. Speaking of which – "You happen to get any I.D.s on those hoods in front of Hollywood High?"

"Right here." I could hear computer keys clicking. "Dan McCallum and Lupe Alonza. Both D.O.A. No I.D. on the driver – toast. You're dangerous around gasoline lately, I notice."

"It's the wind. Raps?"

"Various. Armed robbery and drugs, mostly. Three murder charges, one conviction, for Alonza."

"Affiliations?"

"Nothing clear. But both have worked for the Sandoval organization before."

I pursed my lips. The Sandoval family was one of L.A.'s more prominent criminal organizations. Though they had a number of other income sources, drugs were their main stock in trade. It was a good lead.

"I'll check into that if I have to. Right now, I just want to dump my teenage tagalong." Through the window, I could see Sarah paying for the clothes with the money I'd given her. It was time to move. "Call you later."

"Lucky me," echoed snidely back from the receiver, but I clicked it into the holder. Uppity woman.

47

Sarah emerged from the store as I stepped away from the phone. She was wearing the new outfit and carrying a shopping bag. She had to raise her voice over the blowing wind. "Who were you talking to?"

"My assistant. What's in the bag?"

"My old clothes. You have an assistant?"

I ignored the question, lifting the bag from her grip and tossing it into a nearby trash container. "Lose 'em."

She squealed angrily, lunging after the bag. "Hey! That was my favorite—"

"Dead weight," I snapped, catching her arm. "We've got no way to clean 'em – and in any case, you're enough trouble without luggage. You said your boyfriend had a place in Silverlake. Let's go."

"He's not my boyfriend." She had pulled away, scrabbling in the bag.

"Semantics. Would you get out of there?" The wind caught the shopping bag and blew it away down the street. The morning traffic was starting to pick up and I felt overly exposed.

Sarah pulled a small makeup kit from the pocket of the skirt. She pocketed the compact and dropped the clothes back into the garbage. "How far is it to Silverlake?"

"Couple miles. You never been there?"

"Not during the day." She flipped open the compact, tried to touch up a cheek. The wind blew the powder from her brush.

"Damn."

I reached over and snapped the case closed. "Save it 'til we get there."

She jerked away angrily. "Will you leave me *alone*?" Her voice had the sudden snappish whine of a tired, cranky teenager. I blinked, taking a slow breath as I fought down a rising tide of anger. I felt put-upon and unappreciated. It's probably how parents feel all the time.

But I had an advantage. I would be able to shed my redheaded little albatross in Silverlake, less than an hour away.

"I intend to," I growled. "And the sooner the better." I turned on my heel and stalked away up the streets, the *satana* blowing red dust at my heels.

A moment later, she was panting up behind me, "I'm sorry . . ."

I strode on toward the hills of Silverlake. "Shut up."

6

Reaching Silverlake took a little longer than I expected.
We had to dodge two cruising cop cars and one official-
looking government vehicle that I suspected was FBI. It
had two stolid-looking suits in it; one black, one white.
They were eyeing the streets watchfully, but I had pulled
Sarah hastily around a corner to concealment. Luck and
the Owl's well-enhanced sense of paranoia was keeping
us hidden, but it wouldn't last forever. I kept a forced
pace up into the wind-whipped hills. The sooner I was
free of Sarah the sooner I could vanish for a while. I
even allowed myself the luxury of fantasizing about it
for a bit. An enforced vacation . . . I hadn't been off
the streets in years. A balmy beach in the South Seas
. . . Danny could join me . . . maybe I would even leave
my guns.

The thought made me snort. Fat chance.

Sarah glanced up defensively at the snort. She was leaning
back against a grimy picket fence, panting in the hot wind.
"I'm not used to hills."

I'd barely noticed them, myself. The Owl spends twenty-
four hours a day walking the streets. I have legs like iron,
and endurance to match. I glanced up Montana street.

"Up there?"

She swallowed, trying to stop panting, and gasped.
"Twenty-one forty, yeah."

The hot wind rattled through the overgrown shrubbery,
ivy and begonias fluttering from the snarled branches of the
trees overhead. Silverlake was old semi-elegance; its clutter
of small houses originally built by L.A.'s early aristocrats
to house their servants.

But the aristocrats had long since died; their descendants moving to Beverley Hills and the mansions replaced by office buildings. Now only Silverlake was left, a hilly region of small, well-built houses gradually decaying from neglect. Sarah and I walked up the cracked and uneven sidewalks, the wind in the trees making a sound like waves breaking on a sandy shore.

A vacation . . . Tahiti maybe . . .

"He's got a gun!"

Sarah's words were a shriek, galvanizing my right hand before they even registered in my brain. The lean man with the braided ponytail had stepped from the doorway of the house ahead, silenced Ruger swinging in a silvery arc. *Pok!* He was good. The ·22 hollowpoint slammed into my head and I fell, skull pounding, behind the low brick retaining wall of the sloped yard. I landed on something squishy.

Sarah grunted, gasping and struggling. "Get off!"

Ponytail came down the drive at a fast rush, low and dangerous. His Ruger quested—

I swung my left arm up and shot him over the top of the wall.

Ponytail jerked, rolling for cover behind a new Mustang parked in the driveway. The brief glimpse I had of his face showed only surprise. He peered up again, his pistol ready.

Beneath me, Sarah struggled to breathe. I rolled off her and into a crouch behind the wall, pistols in both hands.

"You shot him with a *BB gun*!?"

"It's a quiet neighborhood," I growled. "Let's keep it that way." My head still ached, but my fiberglass-armored Kevlar cap had stopped the bullet.

"But—"

"Shaddup."

Behind the car, Ponytail suddenly fell down. I moved up fast. The pointed pellet had been packing a crystal of shellfish toxin. Potent stuff. Ponytail was stone dead. He looked more surprised than ever.

"Christ," Sarah gasped behind me. I shoved her away.

"Stay back," I commanded, and moved toward the house at a sprint.

The door was slightly ajar. I hit it with my shoulder and went in at a dive, rolling across the floor and coming up with Peacemaker extended. The first thing I saw was Sarah standing vacantly in the doorway behind me, looking at the ransacked interior in amazement.

"Whoa . . . what d'y'think happened here?" she asked, closing the door.

I didn't answer, because at that moment a heavy-set Hispanic in a suit lunged out of the bedroom with a revolver. *BOOM!* I blew him backwards over a shredded couch and went through the bedroom door at a rush.

Bedroom, bathroom, closet, kitchen. Nobody else. The place looked like it had been run through a garbage shredder. Every stick of furniture had been torn apart. Clothes had been ripped. Even the light fixtures and wall sockets had been wrenched from the plaster.

Sarah stepped gingerly over the body on the floor, looking at the wreckage surrounding.

"You think they were looking for Jason?"

I grimaced, holstering the Peacemaker. "Is he a midget?" She gave me a look. "No."

"Then he's not all they were looking for." I was going through the pockets of the man on the floor. To my surprise, he was carrying I.D. The surprise stopped when I saw his name.

Hector Sandoval.

Now I was *really* in trouble.

7

The police car turned in at the end of the block and accelerated rapidly. Sarah looked back as it turned screechingly on Douglas.

"Was he after us?"

"Somebody probably heard the shooting." I slowed the car, pulling over to the curb. With any luck—

WHUPOOM! A sudden blast of flame and debris erupted from up the hill. I'd kicked the stove's gas connection loose before we'd left, and left a lighted candle in the living room. It had only been a matter of time.

"Holy shit," Sarah gasped, leaning past me to look out the window. "I didn't, like, quite realize—"

"I have a weakness for the spectacular." My eyes were on the cop car. It had screeched to a halt on the hill, the two flabbergasted cops leaping from the interior. With some satisfaction, I noticed that the driver had failed to set the parking brake. The black-and-white began rolling backwards, gaining speed.

I stomped the accelerator, twisted the wheel. We'd taken the two hoods' brand-new Mustang and it had power to spare. The Mustang was out onto Sunset by the time the rolling back-and-white reached the base of Montana. It plowed into an ivy-covered DWP rectifier box with a smash. Sparks flew in the wind as the car crackled and snapped. The cops danced around it, yelling.

Despite my mood, I grinned. Smoke was rolling into the sky from the burning house, and the cops were in no position to stop it. I'd dragged Ponytail's body inside, so any evidence recovered later would be black, crispy, and largely unconclusive. Which is just the way the Owl likes it.

Sarah was still looking back toward the carnage. "You know . . . I was going to ask . . . were you a soldier or something?"

A fair question, and no big secret. I shrugged. "Reporter," I said. "Believe it or not. I worked a plum investigative assignment about ten years back – inside report on a radical paramilitary splinter of the JDL. I had eight months of intensive weapons and terrorist combat training. Turned out I was a natural shot." I laughed wryly at the memory. " 'Course, after all that trouble, my editors never got around to running the article. But what the hell – the training they paid for turned out to be unexpectedly useful."

Sarah's green eyes looked at me sideways. "Yeah . . . I'll say."

Time to change the subject. I fumbled in my pocket, took out a cassette tape. It was a Radio Shack cheapie, marked ICM CASSETTE. Sarah looked at it.

"What's that?"

"Answering machine tape. Our friend with the ponytail had it in his pocket." I slipped the tape into the car's stereo. There was a hiss of leader, then:

"Jason, this is Steve. Gimme a call, okay?" BEEP.

I glanced at Sarah. "Who's Steve?"

She blinked, shook her head. The tape continued; a girl's voice this time. "Jason, it's me. *Please* pick up if you're there. Please?" The voice sounded shaky and scared. There was a frightened pause, and I looked over at Sarah. She didn't meet my gaze. "Allegra," she confirmed in a low voice.

The scared voice continued. "Oh, God. I'm at home. Call me as soon as you get this. *Please.*" BEEP.

I frowned. The next voice was deep but neutral. "Magrina. It's not working. Pick up if you're there . . . Shit." BEEP.

I heard a faint chime in the back of my mind, but the next voice interrupted my train of thought. Allegra again. "Jason, God, *please* call me right away." BEEP.

The machine gave a short series of clicks and beeps, indicating that someone – possibly Allegra – had called and hung up several times more. A few other people called, leaving only their first names. Probably customers. A few more hang-ups. Then came the last message on the tape.

"Hey, dude, this is Steve again. It's Tuesday morning. I hope you get this, 'cause I can't make it to Linoleum tonight. Got a date with Crystal." The voice laughed, a little wildly. "Come on by and we'll celebrate, guy. Anyway, gimme a call."

BEEP.

I popped the tape from the cassette player and tossed it out the window. "Linoleum."

"It's a club or something. I don't know where it is."

"I do." I frowned grimly through the windshield, feeling the hot winds gust against the beefy car. I was still trying to identify that chime in the back of my head. But the fear in Allegra's taped voice kept intruding—

At that moment a buzz sounded from a handheld cellular phone clipped under the dash. Sarah squeaked in surprise. I was surprised myself, but managed to maintain a cool exterior. I reached for the unit, clicked it on.

"You're not going to *answer* it!?"

"Part of the job." The phone crackled static in my ear. "Hello?"

"Sammy?" The voice on the other end had a slight South American accent. "Let me speak to Hector."

Samuel had been the name on Ponytail's ID. Unfortunately, I had never heard him speak. I did the best I could, speaking low and hoping the cellular static would cover for me.

"Hector's not here."

It didn't work. "Who is this? Where's Hector and Sammy?" The voice was suddenly sharp, suspicious. Time to shift the game.

"Both dead," I said cheerfully. "They were careless. You Sandovals gotta get your act together."

The voice grew louder, anger thundering from the handset. "Magrina!"

I said nothing, simply laughed. The voice became a hate-filled snarl.

"You little son of a bitch. You've stepped too far. This power play is now your death sentence. I'll—"

"Owl!" Unfortunately, Sarah had overheard. She was yanking on my arm. "Dammit, stop that! You'll get Jason killed! You—"

Crack! This was no time for niceties. I smacked her back against the car door, red hair flying. She wailed.

"L'Hiboux." The voice in the phone was suddenly cold. "Yes. It is you after all, is it not."

I did my best to sound tough and cool, despite the shuddering girl in the passenger seat. "Confirmed. Who's this?"

"Enrique Sandoval. You have become an unexpected difficulty in an already unfortunate situation."

"I'm good at that."

"I assume you have Sarah Scarlotti in the vehicle with you. You should feel fortunate, since she is keeping you alive at this moment. Hector was not a close relative, but blood must be paid for by blood."

I twisted the wheel, skidding the Mustang over to the curb. Sarah was flung across the seat, landing against me, but she shoved herself away angrily. I wasn't in a mood to explain. I grabbed her by the arm, pulling her bodily from the car. She screamed, the wail resounding quaveringly in the howling wind. I dragged her down the street—

A horn blew. "Hey! hey! Is there some trouble here?"

Another blasted good citizen; a middle-aged man in a middle-aged Toyota, suddenly deciding to be a hero. Pretty girls have this effect. I kicked in his side window for him, glass shattering over the car's interior. "Get the fuck out of here."

I probably looked insane, which was just fine with me. The man's face lost its nerve. "Jesus!" He floored the pedal, his car screeching away.

I still had the phone in one hand and Sarah in the other. I slammed her back against a dusty concrete building and held her there as I put the phone to my ear again and forced my voice down to what I hoped was an icy calm. "So, you were saying?"

The voice chuckled with the wind, angry amusement without humor. "You have left the car."

"Suppose you tell me what's going on."

"It is simple, Mr L'Hiboux. I want the girl. Bring her to me by tomorrow. Or else."

The connection went dead.

And the car blew up.

I half-dragged Sarah rapidly down a side street, shards of metal still rattling to the asphalt behind us. Horns sounded and people shouted, but all the attention was on the detonated car. A wheel rolled by in the distance.

To give her credit, Sarah had stopped struggling when the car exploded. Twenty-four hours with the Owl had at least twigged the bare beginnings of a survival instinct. She followed unprotestingly, though she did give me a reproachful glance as she touched her swollen lip.

"Ow."

"Pipe down." I released her arm, since she was following on her own, and dodged into an alley just off Benton. A pair of Mexican workers were there, repairing a crumbling wall behind an auto-parts shop. They looked up as we approached.

"*Qué pasa, amigos?*" I tossed them the cellular phone, which I was still carrying. "Knock yourselves out. Free calls to Guadalajara or wherever – courtesy of my good friend Enrique."

I took a quick glance back as we reached the far end of the alley. The two men were already tentatively tapping at the buttons.

The wind greeted us with a swirl of dust as we stepped from around the corner. Sarah blinked against the grit, wiping her lips, then wincing. Her voice was subdued.

"You shouldn't make them mad."

"The Sandovals? Old Enrique is already plenty displeased. That car didn't blow up by accident." I was looking around.

We had emerged in a cul de sac just off Westmoreland, a cluster of battered Spanish-style apartments overlooking a dead-end street half-clogged with parked or abandoned cars. The wind blew dust over everything. On normal days, the street would have been a lazy scene of easygoing Hispanics loitering on the steps or working on the cars. But the grit-filled wind had driven them all inside. Sarah and I stood in the shadows of a ghost town.

"Yeah, what *was* that? How did the car blow up?"

"Radio bomb. Sensible business precaution taken by many of your more thoughtful druglords. In case an underling gets arrested or tries a doublecross. Eliminates evidence and/or enemies. Only reason we're still alive is because of you. The Sandovals want you delivered."

Her eyes looked up, frightened. The wind moaned in the empty doorways.

"Are you going to do it?"

"The temptation is growing," I admitted, "but no. I prefer to maintain a rep for not being pushed around by scum."

Her relief was blatant. "Okay, good, then—"

"*On* the other hand." My voice had the gritty edge of the wind blowing around us. "I also want to avoid a reputation for being pushed around by teenage redheads. So shut up. This has gone on long enough. Two houses, a couple of cars, and nine dead bodies – including your parents – all for a lousy quarter million bucks worth of face Drano. This is getting way out of hand. And what really pisses me off is: I'm right in the goddamn *middle* of it and I'm not even getting *paid*." I leaned toward her, glowering for emphasis. It wasn't easy, because she was giving me that scared-kitten look, but I had my shades to hide behind. I managed. "Face it, young lady. Protecting the public is a job for the police, not the Owl. I stepped in because I thought you were in trouble. Now I've got the cops, the Sandovals, and the FBI on my ass, and as far as I can tell, your situation is worse than ever. I'm not doing you any good. So—"

So then she kissed me. Impulsively fast, her arms around my neck and her lips warm against mine. The wind blew around us, swirling her hair against my cheek. It smelled of perfume and exhaustion; femininity mixed with a lingering trace of fear. Her soft tongue swirled through my mouth for the briefest instant—

"Mmphm!" I managed to pull away, straightening angrily. "Goddammit—!" The sudden stiffening in my jeans that her actions had produced only made me more annoyed. I was being blatantly manipulated and I didn't like it.

"I'm *sorry!*" She threw herself against my chest, green eyes filling. "That wasn't fair, I know. But you've saved my life a couple of times already, and all I've done is complain. So I don't blame you for wanting to get rid of me, but please, please don't. I'll try to be better, I swear."

I tried to pull away, but my back was already against the wall. "Let go."

She did so, slowly. I stepped away from the wall, my hands clenched into fists in my pockets. But I kept my voice even.

"To start with, don't try that again. I don't know what you had in mind, but if I want a whore, I pay in cash, not service." Sarah gasped like she'd been struck, but I continued relentlessly. "You're good at manipulating men, I'll give you that. Most girls your age are, but you have a real talent. There's just one problem."

I paused, growling a little. The wind in the empty doorways answered me.

"I am the Owl. I am justice for hire; vengeance at a price. I've killed more men than you would believe – and a number of them died very horribly indeed. I'm a paranoid psychotic with a biological quirk. I never sleep and I never rest. I hunt twenty-four hours a day, seven days a week. Most criminals fear me; the rest of the world doesn't believe I exist. Sometimes, I swear I don't believe it myself. It's not an easy life.

"But one thing keeps me going; one thing keeps me sane. Call it a code of honor. Admittedly, I'm not exactly a model citizen. Despairingly people who are desperate for justice pay me to track down criminal scum and execute them horribly. But I stay true to my code. I've never killed an innocent man – and I've never failed a client. I don't go back on my word or quit a case. And I don't mess with sixteen-year-old girls."

I looked away, across the blowing debris in the empty street. Far away, the wind brought the sound of sirens; emergency vehicles surrounding the exploded car. "I can handle the street life. I can handle the danger. I can handle the killing. But at the age of thirty-two . . . " I looked back at her. "I'm just not ready to feel like a dirty old man."

Sarah had settled to a seated position beside a building's steps, head down, huddled against the hot wind. She was silent for a long moment, then finally looked up seriously.

"Can I say something?"

I nodded. And she stood abruptly.

"It was just a *kiss*, for God's sake. Don't make a federal case out of it." She shook her head dismissively, gesturing up the windblown street. "Now can we go? I'm starved."

She started away, leaving me blinking like a fool. I shook my head, trying to recover. "Hey."

She stopped and looked back. Scarlet hair tousled in the red wind. "What?"

"We'll go to Linoleum tonight. If your boyfriend's there, fine. You can go with him. If not – you go to the police, understand? I'm not a bodyguard. This fiasco has gone on too long already."

Green eyes contemplated me thoughtfully. "Fair enough."

"I should think so," I muttered, following her up the street. I was still stuck with her, still not getting paid. And up to a few minutes ago, I had been planning to turn her over to the cops immediately. She must have sensed it. Because somehow or another, she'd bought herself some time.

The taste was as bitter as the windblown grit in my mouth. *I was still being manipulated.*

8

La Casa de China was a vile place, a Chinese restaurant in a Mexican neighbourhood, and run, oddly enough, by a local gang of Koreans. The place specialized in strange food, beer, and heroin. The dim concrete patio was roofed and shuttered against official eyes, the graffiti-scarred walls dark with smoke and pocked with bullet holes. The hot wind outside whistled through the narrow crevices that served the place for windows, stirring the sluggish mixture of stenches. I took a deep breath. The dimness. It was my kind of place.

As usual, the crowd was almost entirely made up of Mexican males. I pushed my way past a crowded table at which a noisy drug deal was being negotiated over many *cervezas*, heading for the grease-stained ordering window. No one gave me a second glance. My mixed racial heritage and deep-tanned skin allows me to fall naturally within a wide range of ethnic parameters, from light-skinned black to dark-tanned Malibu surfer. With my American Indian bone structure, Hispanic is no problem at all.

Naturally, I was alone. A teenage redheaded Valley girl would have been conspicuous as Hell in this place, and I have an aversion for attention. Especially since the news reports had given the impression that I had kidnapped her. Latins can be unpredictably chivalrous at times. All I needed was to have a gang of drunk, doped-up Mexican drug dealers decide to "rescue" Sarah.

I stepped to the window. Despite all appearances, the food here was pretty good, though unusual. Things like burrito-stuffed eggrolls and Korean tacos with *kim chee* garnish adorned the menu. The surly, tough-looking Korean inside the sweltering kitchen squinted at me through the greasy smoke. He looked more irritable than usual. The wind was getting to him even in there.

"*Dos* eggrolls, Coca-cola *grande*," I said, pointing at the menu mounted beside the window and indicating the choices with the proper amount of fingers. Language didn't matter here. As far as anyone had ever discovered, the cook spoke no languages at all. Pointing was good enough.

The cook nodded sourly, throwing some white cylinders into a bubbling vat of brown grease. I started to reach for my wallet – and paused. Like an old-time Western movie, the noisy room behind me had suddenly gone dead silent.

I didn't turn around, didn't move. Two pairs of heavy feet walked toward my back, the leather soles sticking on the filthy concrete. They stopped.

"Alexander L'Hiboux?" The voice was a bit nasal, with an East Coast accent.

FBI. Had to be. No LAPD cop would have been stupid enough to enter *La Casa de China* without two squads of backup. It took the Federal government to be this boneheaded. I didn't turn around.

"L'Hiboux!"

This time I turned around, with an air of vacant curiosity; just an everyday citizen wondering what the noise was about. I faced a couple of stolid, middle-aged suits. One was white, of chunky build and short-cropped hair. The other was leaner and black. They were the same ones I had spotted earlier in the car. This time they had spotted me. Their hands rested inside their jackets, gun butts protruding. Around them, the swarthy crowds watched in tense silence. Watched *me*. They had recognized the name. Near the back of the room, I saw a bet being made.

"*Lo siento,*" I said. "*Me habla?*"

The Feds blinked, faces blank. Their Spanish was limited, if they knew any at all. The chunky one frowned.

"Cut the crap and speak English." He produced a leather folder, flipped it open to show his badge. "Agents Scale and Gordon, FBI. Let's see some I.D."

I felt almost annoyed. Years of hard work had gone into building the Owl's reputation, and yet these two seemed to have memorized nothing more than my physical description. The rest of the room tittered in anticipation. The Owl had been invited to reach into his jacket. Surreptitious bets increased as the onlookers prepared to dive for the floor.

I felt bad having to disappoint my fans, but the Owl does not kill lawmen, no matter the temptation. All I produced from my jacket was my wallet. "Of course," I replied, flipping it open. But from it I abruptly produced a sheaf of bills, holding them up as my voice suddenly thundered in Spanish: *"Five hundred dollars to the first gun I see!"*

It was close, I have to admit it, but the kid in front with the silver ·380 was just a shade faster than the others. The room was a sudden forest of cocked handguns, and they were all pointed at the stunned Feds.

"Gracias." I complacently tossed a wad of green on the kid's table. None of the guns moved as I swiftly used the agent's own cuffs to bind their hands. The two Feds were livid, shaking with fury. Scale's voice was a snarl.

"You're making a serious mistake, L'Hiboux. *Very* serious."

I tightened his cuffs an extra notch. "I'll be up nights, worrying."

A sudden shove sent them both to the floor, sprawling in the beer-sodden filth. The room's occupants crowded around them, leering meaningfully. It was a terrifying sight, but the Feds were tough. Gordon fixed me with an icy glance.

"Don't be stupid, L'Hiboux. Killing us will just make things worse for you."

I smiled easily. "I don't see how," I said. "However, I have no intention of killing you." Glancing at the others, I switched to Spanish. "Strip them. Take what you want, then turn them loose. Don't hurt them, just humiliate them. They will not dare report it. And there will be no investigation of this incident."

The crowd laughed, a bone-chilling sound. They reached for the agents. Knives were produced, steel gleaming in the darkness. There was a tearing of cloth and startled curses from the agents. I gave them an insolent salute.

"Welcome to L.A.," I said, and turned away. My eggrolls were ready.

9

I had left Sarah a block away, at the corner of Vermont and Franklyn. It was a strangely upscale little area, a last oasis of what was once a fashionable L.A. nightspot. But these days, the local residents were no longer of a class able to afford such luxuries. Thus, the elderly clubs were slowly sinking beneath an encroaching mass of *barrios*, urban blight, and 7-elevens.

The searing wind puffed grit from the ageing brick, swirling papers and leaves around the feet of the few irritated-looking pedestrians. A bag lady shuffled by, swearing ceaselessly in a senile, muttering undertone. I felt the same way. The sun was hot, red and merciless above. I had already unzipped the sleeves from my battle jacket again, stowing them in a rear pouch. Squinting through my sunglasses, I surveyed the almost barren streets.

Sarah was gone.

I cursed inwardly and began moving along the sidewalk fast. Up ahead, at the corner of Russell, a police black-and-white was parked. My instincts told me to vanish. I told my instincts to shut up.

The car was empty. I stepped cautiously around the corner – and practically bumped into two cops stepping out of a frozen yoghurt store. Engrossed in their yoghurt cups, which were already dripping in the heat, they gave me only a brief glance of irritation. I moved away, up the street. They got back into their car and drove slowly away.

"Owl!" A cheery musical shout, resounding over the wind. Sarah was emerging from the glass door of the post office across the street. "Over here!"

She couldn't have been louder or anything, could she? In a half-panic, I scanned the streets. Luckily, they were pretty much deserted of pedestrians, and the cars all had their windows shut against the blowing dirt. I made a short, angry "keep it *down*" gesture across the street and Sarah stopped waving abruptly. She almost looked apologetic as I hustled up to her.

"I'm sorry – I forgot."

"Mistakes like that get people killed," I snarled in annoyance. "What the hell were you doing in there?"

"Just getting out of the wind, you know? Besides, I saw those cops. I was watching for you, though." She noticed the bag of burrito-stuffed eggrolls I was carrying. The grease was by now leaking through the bottom. "Eeeeww. What's that?"

"Food," I said shortly, producing one of the greasy rolls. "Street food. Out here, you eat when you can; sometimes just once a day. You want simple food with a lotta calories; mostly proteins and fats with carbos to burn. To Hell with vegetables and fiber. Taking a dump out here is no easy task. You don't want to encourage it."

Sarah had broken the end of her eggroll open, peering inside with distaste. "Looks like somebody did it right in here." She took a tentative bite. "Tastes okay, though."

"It should. They cost enough," I muttered.

"What?"

"Nothing. Hurry up and eat. I've got to stop by the bank."

"The Owl has a bank account?"

"Stop *broadcasting*." The only one in earshot was an elderly derelict, who despite the heat was huddled in a heavy coat. Blood thinned by alcohol. "Not under my own name, of course. But yeah. Quite a few actually. Let's go."

Sarah followed me down the street, suddenly pensive. "Owl – I mean, Alex?"

"Now what?"

"Um . . . How *do* you . . . I mean, how do I · . . . um . . . "

"Spit it out."

"I gotta go poop."

"Right." My look was bemused, but I kept walking. "You're a little green yet for the old 'back against the wall' manuever. Also, you're reasonably well-dressed, and it's daytime. There's a few tricks . . . "

"Service station?"

I snorted. "In L.A.? You'd have better luck finding a doctor that made house calls. No." I nodded at a tall building down the street, faintly visible through the wind-blown dust. "The bank's just ahead. We'll take care of you there."

We dodged cop cars to the bank building, walking half a block apart to reduce suspicion. I used the automatic teller to replenish my wallet, praying that Danny had buried the account deep enough to avoid the FBI. But the teller disgorged the cash without incident. I got it into my wallet without the wind snatching it away and we went on into the building.

The bank took up one half of the lower floor, glass windows looking into the lobby. There was a pair of restrooms visible in one wall. Sarah tried the womans' door. "It's locked."

"Naturally. Don't want bums using it. Come on." I led the way to the building directory, scanning it quickly. "It'll be the same on the first couple of floors. Street people sometimes wander up there. After about the fourth floor, though, it's not often a problem. And the tenants get tired of always having to find their keys every time nature calls. So they start leaving the restroom doors unlocked."

We stepped to the elevator, which opened at the touch of a call button. Sarah followed me in.

"Let's go to the top, then."

"Nope." My finger punched a button. "That's all one company. They'll probably have a receptionist right by the elevator. We want a floor with about four different companies – here. Sixth floor."

As I predicted, we looked out on a blank hallway, smelling slightly of carpet adhesive and stale air conditioning. A man carrying a file of papers barely glanced at us as he stepped into the elevator we had just left. The door *dinged* and he was gone.

Sarah had already moved hastily down the hallway, pulling open the door of the woman's restroom. "Thank God."

"I'll wait," I said, but she had vanished inside with a touch of telltale speed.

Actually, as long as I was there . . . and the men's room was only a few feet away . . .

One of the stalls was occupied when I went in, but there were two others to choose from. On one of them someone had experienced an exceptional bowel movement and, obviously proud of the achievement, had left it for others to admire. I took the other stall.

For most people, there are few better places than this for deep thought, and the Owl is no exception. Thoughts and flashes of memory swirled in my brain. The past twenty-four hours or so had been busy indeed – but something wasn't adding up. Too much activity, too many people going to too much trouble over a mediocre six-pound coke ripoff. Even escalating revenge didn't explain enough. There was more to it than that, a missing piece . . .

Someone else had entered the bathroom, whistling. I heard him glance into the unoccupied stall and retch slightly, then pause a moment as he contemplated the others. He would have to wait.

Except he didn't. He kicked open the stall next to mine and blew away the guy inside.

I was becoming attuned to the silenced "*phut!*" of a Sandoval hitman. Their organization must buy Ruger ·22s by the gross. They are quiet and effective, but have difficulty penetrating stainless-steel toilet stalls. The assassin had to kick the doors open. I had no such handicap.

BOOMBOOMBOOMBAROOM! The Peacemaker bucked and roared, the giant ·45 slugs tearing fist-sized holes in the brushed stainless doors. I was firing blind, aiming by ear and instinct, the big Colt's blast painful in the closed tile bathroom. Blood sprayed under the door.

Wrenching the door open, I lunged out low. The dark-haired torpedo was sprawled in a bloody heap against the sink, two bullet holes in him but fury in his eyes. He aimed his pistol at my face and pulled the trigger.

The flash burned my eyes, but the bullet missed. I would like to say the Owl's catlike reflexes were responsible, but in truth, I had tripped over the pants which were still around my ankles. I rolled across the tile floor as he struggled to aim another shot. He didn't get one. The Peacemaker kicked hard against my hand, and the mirror behind his head shattered – painted with red.

I heard screams – and one of them was familiar. I was sprinting from the bathroom before I'd even gotten my pants up.

The second assassin was dragging Sarah from the woman's bathroom at gunpoint, Sarah screaming her head off. The assassin belted her with the pistol. I swung up the Peace-maker – and froze.

The assassin was a woman.

And a darn good-looking woman, too. One of those smoldering Latin types; tall, dark, and dangerous with curves like the Andes mountains and eyes like pools of smoke. Holding Sarah before her like a shield, she was trying to aim her pistol at me. But I was behind the cover of a drinking fountain alcove, and Sarah's struggles were making it difficult to draw a bead.

I was in a quandry. What with one thing and another, I had never shot a female before. Only one woman had ever died at the Owl's hands; a death that had changed my life forever. The Peacemaker was cocked, but I couldn't bring it to bear. In my mind, I could still see the flames, hear the screaming . . .

I yanked myself back. It was Sarah doing the screaming here, accompanied by several terrified secretaries gaping from doorways down the hall. The raven-haired torpedo snarled.

"Where's Marco?" Her voice was as hot as her eyes.

"He should have picked door number three." I kept my voice icy to conceal the turmoil in my brain. "How'd you find us?"

The full lips twisted in killer amusement. "We bank here too. Put down your gun. I take the *chiquita*."

"No."

Her response was a bullet, but Sarah's struggles spoiled her aim. The slug punched through my Levis and buried itself in the carpet. My leg burned, a red stain swelling. And the Peacemaker roared.

Ka-TANG! The Ruger spun from the assassin's hand, spinning away through an open office door. It had been a stupid shot to try, since it was my last bullet, but I had gotten lucky. I lunged down the hallway, trying to ignore the fire in my leg.

The woman screamed in fury as I sailed into her, knocking Sarah away. She hit the floor hard with me on top, a sensation I would have enjoyed more if she hadn't immediately kneed me in the groin. My balls smashed against my pelvis and my stomach tried to punch through the top of my head. Dazed, I struggled to hold her down, but she produced an ivory switchblade, flipping it open. She brought it up in a short, ripping arc—

Phutphutphut! The beautiful, furious face below me suddenly sprouted red blossoms. The blade in her hand raked along my battle jacket, sunk lightly into my left arm, then fell to the floor. She was dead.

And Sarah was holding the smoking Ruger, a look of vacant horror on her face.

"Oh, God . . . " she whispered. "I did it." The pistol tumbled from her fingers to the floor. And she burst into tears.

There was no time for this. Holstering the empty Peacemaker, I snatched up the Ruger and swung Sarah over my shoulder. At the far end of the hall, a worried-looking manager-type was peering timidly from a doorway. I sprinted toward him.

He saw me coming and blenched, trying to shut the door. I hit it with my stabbed shoulder, sending him flying over a desk. There was a flurry of screams and fluttering papers as underlings dived for cover, but I ignored them. The Ruger spat rapidly in my hand.

Twenty feet away, the floor-to-ceiling windows starred and split as the ·22 slugs smashed through. Safety glass is tough, but once cracked, it's vulnerable. I went through with my head down and my knees up, Sarah still draped screamingly over my shoulder.

Six stories up, we went sailing out into space.

10

The parking structure behind the building was four stories tall, with cars lining the roof. We fell fifteen feet in a wind-whipped shower of glass and crashed down upon the roof of a late-model BMW. Its alarm blared. Fortunately, this sound is so common in Los Angeles that no one paid any attention.

We had a few seconds. Policemen, summoned by the shooting, were already racing into the front of the building. Squad cars were skidding to a halt in the street. Fortunately, however, the building's bulk had so far concealed our exit. I rolled painfully from the BMW roof, swung the hyperventilating Sarah over my shoulder once more, and ran limpingly for the stairwell. The wind buffeted me with gusts of heat, swirling fragments of shattered glass from my clothes. Staggering into the urine-scented stairwell, I set Sarah down on her feet.

"Can you walk?" I panted.

She nodded, breathless and dazed, but upright. I kept a hand on her arm as we clattered down the stairwell. Blood dripped from my leg on the stained iron steps. Sarah noticed it and gasped.

"You're hurt!"

"I'll live." The wound was a clean, shallow puncture in my outer right thigh, severing no major arteries. It hurt like hell and bled oozingly, but I gritted my teeth on the pain. I pushed the stairwell's ground floor door open and stepped out. Sarah followed.

"Which way?"

"Not this way. They'll expect this. I just wanted to leave a blood trail." Drops of crimson were already staining the

72

windswept concrete. I reached for Sarah's shirttail and ripped it off. "Pardon me."

With the shirt as a crude tourniquet, I stopped the bleeding and shoved Sarah back into the stairwell. From high in the distance, I could hear commands being shouted from the building's shattered window. We had to move fast.

The parking structure had an underground area, used mainly by monthly rentals. The line of cars within were expensive, luxurious – and equipped with sophisticated anti-theft devices. I ignored them. What I was heading for was a simple circle of pierced metal, set in the lowest part of the floor.

Sarah blinked as I set my fingers in the cover's holes and lifted. "Down the sewer?"

"Storm drain." The metal cover grated open and I set it to one side. Rust-covered metal rungs embedded in concrete led into the dimness below. "Get going. Hurry."

She had long since learned not to argue. Footsteps rattled on the floors above, sirens sounding in the distance. I followed her painfully down the ladder and slid the corroded lid closed behind us. A fine powder of iron oxide rained down on my head, the color of dried blood.

Even down here, you could feel the wind. It whistled through the curb grates, gusted through the darkened tunnels. It tugged the hairs at the back of my neck with a feeling of tight unease. Sarah was waiting for me in the darkness at the bottom of the ladder. She pressed up against me, warm and timid. I didn't push her away.

She squeaked slightly as my pencil flash cut through the darkness. It was only a tiny Mag-Light, but the beam it cast was a reassuring torch. I played it around a moment.

I've been in sewers before. By contrast, these older L.A. storm drains are positively swank. Tall enough to stand up in and fully six feet wide, they resemble concrete hallways with a ditch on the middle. The ditch was dry now, the hot air smelling only faintly of garbage and decay.

73

But there was gang graffiti on the walls, plenty of it. I eased Sarah away and began jacking spent shells from the Peacemaker.

"What's wrong?" Her eyes were big, looking around worriedly. Even in the darkness, I could tell she was growing paler, her hands shook.

"Nothing yet," I mumbled. I was holding the flashlight in my teeth. Dropping the brass in my pocket, I led the way west, our footsteps echoing hollowly against the concrete. "Just have to reload."

We stepped out into a broad, circular storm drain junction. Three tunnels led out of it, including the one we had just come from. Narrow beams of hot, dusty light pierced redly down from holes in an overheat vent cover, dimly illuminating the graffiti-scrawled chamber with blood-colored light. And six fat ·45 rounds slid with solid thumps into the Peacemaker's chambers. I gave the cylinder a spin, lowered the hammer to the half-cock safety, and slid the big pistol back into its holster. I felt better. Much better indeed.

Sarah wasn't, though. The shaking had increased and she couldn't stop it. I wasn't surprised. Twenty-four hours with the Owl had shown her quite a few bodies, but the last one she had killed herself. And now the truth of it was setting in. Her voice was a keening whisper. "*Oh God oh God oh God oh God . . .* "

She staggered, lost in her own mind, ten feet beneath the East Hollywood streets. She bumped against me, clutched for comfort – then just as abruptly shoved herself away again. The Owl could give no comfort. Not for this.

Overhead, cars thrummed on the asphalt, the wind whistled through the vent holes, and the heat beat its sweltering way clear down into our chamber. We were standing in dimness; hot, moaning, rumbling . . . tinted with blood. And Sarah had shot a woman and watched her die.

She didn't scream this time. Screams were for anguish, for loneliness and despair. She had screamed when her parents died. This was different. I watched without speaking, my hands in my pockets. I knew what she was going through.

74

Something happens the first time you have to kill another human. An empty, aching terror yawns like a sudden abyss in your mind and soul, and you realize that, somehow, you have changed. Utterly and permanently changed. Frighteningly greater than losing virginity, it is more closely akin to birth. You have killed. You have opened a door that can never again be closed and come face to face with a side of yourself that you never admitted, only feared. You see the dark depths in your own soul and react with horror: *My God! Look what I am capable of doing!*

There are three ways of dealing with horror. The first is denial. *It didn't happen, it was an accident, it wasn't real!* Seek comfort in a loved one's arms, try to forget. You can try. But you never will.

The second is transference. *It wasn't me! It was the booze, the circumstances, somebody else!* Keep pushing the reality off, keep it away. It doesn't work. The truth will remain like a nagging splinter in your mind, forever reminding you that you are not what you believe.

The last is acceptance. *Yes. I killed. I killed because I had to.* It is a hard thing to come to terms with. But with it comes calmness, and a certain resignation. *It happened. Let's face it. I had to kill someone, and I did.*

But the hardest realization of all follows soon after. It is never spoken; hardly even thought. But it creeps into your mind anyway, a cold and final truth.

And if I ever had to, I could do it again.

Had Sarah been able to go home, she could have chosen denial. Climbed into her bed, been hugged by her mother, called a few friends, pretended it never happened. But she wasn't at home, and her parents were dead.

At a word from me, she might have transferred. I could have taken some responsibility, helped ease her trauma a little. But the short-term relief would have been paid for in lifelong nightmares. The gun had been in her hand, her finger had pulled the trigger. There was no way she could get around it. So I said nothing. Just stood like a stone statue,

75

watching her. Blood dripped slowly from my leg to the rank concrete floor.

Sarah had sunk slowly to the cement, her back against one wall and a tiny, stagnant puddle at her feet. The puddle, part of a trickle from one of the drains, was visibly evaporating in the hot, dry air. Sarah's head dropped between her knees, her eyes on her own dim reflection in the slowly shrinking puddle.

We remained that way for a long time. Me standing, Sarah sitting, staring at her own reflection. The dry wind moaned through the dimness. The puddle shrank, became nothing but a wet stain on the concrete, and then finally vanished altogether.

Slowly, Sarah looked up. Her eyes sought my arm, looking at my bloodstained shirtsleeve. The gash had stopped bleeding, but it was messy. If the knife had penetrated much deeper, the main artery would have been cut. And the female assassin would have kept cutting, right into my neck.

But she hadn't. Because of Sarah.

The little redhead's eyes shifted, looking at my face, seeking some sort of reassurance. I stayed impassive. However she dealt with it, she would have to do so on her own. At long last, she exhaled heavily and rubbed her face.

"Shit."

A good word: a word long associated with hard truths. It is often the last word heard on the "black box" recordings of crashed aircraft. And Sarah's voice held the same tone of resignation. I nodded.

"Ready to go on?"

Her sigh was long and a little shaky, but she got unsteadily to her feet. "I guess. Which way?"

I looked at her. "You choose," I said.

She blinked, looking dazedly around the junction chamber at the three storm tunnels leading away. Then her gaze steadied, resolute. A glimmering beam of scarlet sunlight spired through a drain vent. Through the dust and wind, it illuminated a tunnel mouth in blood-colored light. "That way."

"Let's go." We walked together into the crimson tunnel, side-by-side, neither speaking. But her head was raised, shoulders back.

She was going to be all right.

Sort of.

All we needed was a little break.

Unfortunately, we didn't get one.

11

We had been walking for maybe a mile, following the convoluted turns of the storm drain system in a southeastern direction. It was dark, dry and desolate. Only the rattle of windblown litter was clearly audible over the wind and the ceaseless thrum of traffic overhead.

Yet suddenly Sarah turned around. "Somebody's behind us."

I had heard it too: a faint steady patter of shoes, suppressed laughter. Three, maybe more, coming up fast. They knew we were here.

They knew the tunnels, too. We rounded a corner and stopped. Thirty feet ahead, the drain tunnel ended abruptly. Reddish sunlight streamed through a street grate, but there was no ladder. The only way out was back the way we had come.

And the footsteps were almost upon us.

I moved back to the corner, fast and silent. From the other side, I heard the *snicks* of several switchblades clicking open. This was followed by a short whisper, and a *schick-schick*. One of them was working the slide on a cheap automatic.

Gang. Okay, I could deal with that.

The one with the gun came first. He was a black teenager, easing around the corner with the gun pointed upward in front of his face, a classic Hollywood pose. Unfortunately for him, that pose looks better than it functions. I slammed the heel of my hand forward, bashing the pistol against the bridge of his nose. *BLAM!* The auto roared loudly in the concrete tunnel, the bullet ripping a groove in his forehead and the recoiling slide practically tearing off his lower lip.

He dropped the gun and screamed, holding his face.

There were three others, lunging forward fast. They all had blades. I grabbed the nearest one by the wrist and brought it down hard as my knee came up. His elbow snapped across my thigh even as I spun.

I took a knife in the back as I belted the third across the face and kicked him in the groin. There was a curse behind me as I felt the cheap steel snap against the Kevlar jacket, then I brought my elbow back hard. Teeth crunched behind me, and pain shot up my funnybone. I'd forgotten I wasn't wearing the protective sleeves.

It was enough, though. Two of them were down, and the one with the broken teeth sat heavily, holding a bleeding mouth. The one I'd kicked staggered gamely forward again, knife slashing wildly. I just sidestepped, drawing the Peacemaker. A bash across the base of his skull with the heavy barrel and he dropped beside the others. I kept the Peacemaker in my hand and pointed it at them calmly.

"Move and die," I said.

"You fuckin' muther *fucker*!" The one with the snapped elbow was the only one who could talk at the moment. His voice was an accusing wail. "You broke my mutherfuckin' *arm*!"

Sarah stepped quietly up behind me. "You're lucky to be alive, dummy. This man is the Owl."

The change in expression was both flattering and disturbing. To street scum like these gang punks, the Owl was a legend, feared yet admired. I hated to be idolized by the type of people I often had to eliminate, but human nature is strange. I could tell the punk was suddenly almost thrilled. To have an arm broken by the Owl would be considered a gang status symbol. He would be a subject of much envy.

"No fuckin' shit?" he breathed. "God damn if it ain't. Shit." There was something else in his expression too, a touch of regret. "An' you mus' be the redhead bitch. Damn, I wish we'd knowed."

Sarah looked puzzled, but I felt my guts tighten. I knew. "What's the price?"

The punk grinned. "For the bitch, twenty-five alive. For yo' ass – a big C on ice. Sandoval be *pissed* at you, bro."

One hundred thousand dollars for the Owl's head. And another twenty-five for Sarah brought in alive. Not a bad price in a city where the average contract hit ran a mere five hundred bucks. The escalation was getting serious. We'd already had the police, the FBI and the Sandovals on our tail. Now they would be joined by every petty criminal and gangbanger on the L.A. streets.

Tahiti was beginning to look better and better.

I didn't let it show on my face, though. The other injured punks were starting to pay attention and the Owl has a reputation to maintain. I sneered instead. "Stick to the lottery. You'll have more chance to collect."

The punk with the busted teeth glared at me with eyes as hot as the wind. "You really that good, mutherfucker?" His voice was slurred and bloody, but edged with anger.

I just gave him an icy glare and replaced the Peacemaker in my shoulder holster. Taking Sarah by the arm, we started away, back up the tunnel. There was silence behind us – then a swift rustle. The punk with the broken teeth dived for the cheap automatic.

BOOOM! Before he'd even swung it up I'd spun, the big Colt leaping into my hand. The punk's face imploded around a sudden central cavity, the back of his head blasting outward in a splattering hail of red. The cheap Llama ·32 arced into the air as he hurtled backward, and my left palm slammed the hammer. *BOOM!BOOOM!BOOOM!* The flimsy auto spun and kicked in the air as the first two slugs hit it, then shattered to bits on the third. Steel shards rained down on a field of blood and skull fragments already coating the concrete floor. I spun the Peacemaker and held it up. Red light poured through a grate behind me and smoke from the barrel drifted around my head. I fixed the other punks with a steady gaze from behind my shades.

"Yeah," I said. "I'm that good."

Sarah and I walked away again, vanishing into the tunnels. Behind us, there was nothing but silence.

12

The sun was setting in a heaving sea of scarlet clouds when we finally emerged from the storm drain. A quick peek from under the manhole cover had shown that we were in a fairly secluded residential alley just above Melrose. I climbed out, grunting. My injured leg was beginning to stiffen and my arm hurt. I had used additional strips of cloth torn from Sarah's shirt to rebandage the wounds, but the result was temporary at best. It also revealed far more of Sarah's lithe, tanned midriff than I was comfortable with. She climbed tiredly from the hole after me and I shoved the cover back into place. No one had seen us, but we were both dirty, tired and disheveled-looking. We needed a convenient place where we could clean up and get a change of clothes. Fortunately, it only took a couple of blocks to find.

"What, you got friends here?" Sarah's ponytail had pulled loose through the day's activities, and the wind tossed her scarlet hair around her face. We were on the second floor of a Polynesian-styled apartment building, the hallway open to the air, California-style.

"Of course not." I bent over the Yale lock, my hands busy with a couple of small spring steel picks. I'm not real good with locks, but I got lucky with this one. It opened almost immediately, and Sarah looked impressed.

"Whoa. Good job."

"Thanks." I pushed the door open cautiously, glancing swiftly around the interior. Expensively furnished but no alarm. I gestured Sarah inside, keeping an eye out for witnesses. Fortunately, the gritty wind was keeping most good citizens inside. I shut the door and relocked it, stopping Sarah as she reached for a switch.

"No lights. Someone might notice."

She took her hand away, looking nervously around the darkened room. "What if whoever lives here comes home?"

"Their mailbox downstairs was stuffed. They've been gone a couple days at least." I took off my sunglasses, nodding at a few European travel brochures scattered around the glass-topped dining table. "Probably overseas. They won't be back for a while. The two last names on the mailbox were different, indicating the likelihood of a fairly young couple. This apartment is not cheap, and neither are the furnishings. Therefore, they make good money. But since they haven't invested it in a house, they are probably spending it pretty freely. Considering the area, they probably go out a lot. Thus, we ought to be able to find something you can wear to the club tonight."

Sarah had listened to my deductions with eyebrows raised admiringly. "You're quite a detective."

Basic reporter training. Observations and conclusions. "Thank you."

"But you're wrong."

"What?"

Sarah picked up a framed photo from a Scandinavian coffee table and handed it to me with a wink. "I might have a *little* trouble finding an outfit," she said. "First dibs on the bathroom."

She pushed past me, and I glanced at the photo. It showed two slim young men at Disneyland smiling at the camera. They were wearing Mickey Mouse ears and embracing fondly.

I sighed and peeled off the heavy battle jacket. The twin shoulder holsters swung ponderously under my arms.

Hell, I'd been *mostly* right.

I cleaned up in the spotless kitchen, rendering it somewhat less spotless. Immaculate dishcloths did good service as bandages, and a clearly-marked first-aid kit supplied both antiseptic and adhesive tape. Off in the bathroom, I could hear the shower start, Sarah humming melodiously behind the closed door.

I tried not to think about it. Tearing off the adhesive tape with my teeth, I bound a pad of cloth to my arm . . .

Scream! Sarah's shriek was an undulating cry of pure terror. I went through the bathroom door like a six-foot cannonball, adhesive tape flying and the Peacemaker cocked in my fist.

Sarah was cowering in a corner, pointing with horror into the shower. I swung the Colt in that direction, but couldn't see a damn thing. "What!?"

"A spider! A big spider—!"

I blinked at her, saying nothing. She looked a bit sheepish. "It went down the drain."

I nodded, still saying nothing, and lowered the Peacemaker's hammer. Turning, I excited the bathroom, shutting the damaged door carefully behind me. I had hit it with my injured shoulder, which now burned like fire. But I barely noticed.

She hadn't been wearing a damn thing.

Outside, the hot wind hooted and chuckled, hurling dust and grit against the window. I felt twitchy, prickly all over. I went to the kitchen and put my head under the tap.

It wasn't a cold shower. But it was the best I could do.

The apartment had only one bedroom, but it had two full armoires. I opened the one belonging to the taller of the two gay men. From the looks of things, he had an inch or so on me, but wasn't as heavy. I selected the loosest pair of designer jeans I could find and tried them on. Not a bad fit, once I had trimmed the legs down with my throwing knife. The dress shirt was snug across the chest, but tolerable. I strapped the knife's arm-sheath to my left forearm and buttoned the sleeve over it. The extra length gave it a concealing volume.

I was shrugging into the twin shoulder holsters when Sarah came in, wrapped in a towel. She nodded, eying my clothes. "Casual, but dressy in a conservative way. The weapons are a daring fashion risk."

I didn't answer, since I was trying to keep my memory from filling in what the towel was concealing. Sarah went to the other armoire, examining the wardrobe within. The shorter of our absentee hosts was something of a flashy dresser. I cleared my throat. "Anything you can use?"

"Oh, sure. Girls get more leeway." She glanced over at me, fingering the towel. "Going to stay?"

I fought down a decidedly uncool flush. "No. Just stay clear of spiders." I left the room, reversing my battle jacket to the black side and putting it on. With the sleeves gone, it more resembled a safari vest and gave the impression I was a photographer. It still hid the shoulder holsters and armored most of the vital organs. My leg and arm were still aching and sore, but I ignored them. I'd already taken some asprin in the kitchen. Replacing the sunglasses and cap, I checked myself in a cut-glass designer mirror. The Owl was ready for action again.

At that moment, there was a *thump* from the rear balcony.

I sprinted toward the noise on my toes, the Peacemaker in my fist. A shadowy figure was on the apartment's rear balcony, holding a small crowbar. Through the gauzy curtains of the dining area, I could barely make out another figure clambering up over the balcony's iron rail.

I snorted and put the Peacemaker away.

Sarah looked startled as I yanked open the bedroom door. She was wearing a tuxedo shirt and a silver lamé bow tie, a silver belt cinching the waist like a minidress. "What—?"

I put a finger to my lips. "We have to go. Now."

"They came back?" The voice was suddenly scared.

I chuckled. From the dining area, I could hear the grating sound of clumsy crowbar work on a sliding glass doorframe. "Nope. Just burglars. Let's clear out."

Sarah snatched up her shoes and a hairbrush from the dresser. "Okay."

We slipped silently out the front door as we heard the sliding glass door shatter at the back. The idiots had gotten frustrated. I heard a muffled exclamation as one cut himself fumbling for the latch. I shut the door on his curses.

Together, Sarah and I walked out into the night, the hot wind a chuckling imp in the darkness. Sarah had to hold the lower end of the tuxedo shirt down as we descended the stairs.

"I wish I had some makeup."

"What happened to your compact?"

"I lost it somewhere. There was some in the bathroom, but not my colors."

"Tsk-tsk. Shame on our absentee hosts."

I left her at the lower step to don her shoes. I went to the apartment door marked "Manager" and rang the bell. After a few moments, a peephole opened and a suspicious eye looked out. "Yeah?"

"I was just walking by," I said pleasantly, "and I happened to notice a couple of people breaking into the back of apartment 204. You might want to call the police."

The eye shifted upward toward the apartment, narrowing angrily. "Yeah. Yeah, I'll do that right now, God dammit. They hit *my* place last week. Thanks, buddy."

"Just a citizen's duty," I assured him, and collected Sarah on my way back out to the sidewalk. She gave me a disbelieving look.

"Hey," I said. "They're *criminals*."

13

It was almost eight o'clock by the time Sarah and I reached the west end of Melrose. The place was lit up like a circus. Neon boutiques, trendy restaurants, art galleries and upscale nightclubs lined both sides of the streets. Music, noise and traffic were thick in the hot, windy night. In a place like this, the Santa Ana was a stimulant, an irritant rush like spicy Thai or a noseful of toot. It gave an unusual feeling of excitement to a Tuesday night, a feeling that something was about to happen. People rushed from boutique to boutique, restaurant to nightclub, laughing, shouting over the wind, getting into sudden arguments about nothing. Out in the street, a fistfight erupted between two young men over a parking space. Their dates sat in the cars, blocking traffic and cheering. I grinned as I watched. Neither kid could fight worth a damn. While they scuffled, a pair of leather-clad bikers stole the parking space.

WHOOP! A warning burst from a police siren scattered the combatants. A cruising black-and-white was coming up the street. I slid quietly into the shadows of a restaurant awning, hoping that Sarah would do the same.

No such luck. A half-block ahead, she had stopped, girlishly entranced by a brightly lit fashion boutique. The cops eased over to a red curb, the shotgun rider leaning from the window. He was holding a copy of the newspaper photo in his hand. "Hey. Miss."

From my vantage point, I watched with mixed emotions. Chief among them was relief. Sarah was in no danger from the cops. I had no fondness for the vanished Jason and didn't particularly care whether he was safe or not. On the other hand, I hated to simply hand a client over to the police, asked for or not. I had struck a deal – to get her as far as the nightclub – and I intended to keep it. I glanced around for a rock. Smashing one of the windows across the street ought to be a reasonable distraction . . .

But I had reckoned without Sarah herself. At the cop's second hail, she had turned. Her expression was simply one of cheerful girlish interest. Had probably spotted the fuzz in the window reflection, and had a second to prepare. A chunk of brick in my hand, I simply watched as she bounced helpfully over to the cop car. The wind blew the officer's words away from me, but I assumed he was asking for I.D. Sarah's response was a nonchalant gesture.

"What, I'm sixteen, you know? And I can't drive yet – I'm just here with my big sister and her boyfriend." A vague gesture at the surrounding shops. "They wanted to try on some geeky clothes, so I said I'd meet them in an hour. That's okay, right? I mean, curfew's not until ten, right?"

The cop was barely listening, studying the photo. He asked her name, asked her to spell it. I could tell she had to fight down the temptation to go with "Scarlet Serenade", but her hesitation was barely noticeable. "Terri Semper," she said, spelling it crisply. Probably a friend. Then she leaned forward, looking at the photo the cop was holding. "Oh, that's that girl, right? The one that got kidnapped? God, you don't think I look like *her*, right? Gross me, I mean, look at her. What a cow."

The cop frowned, still looking doubtful. Fortunately, at that moment, the wind took a hand. Across the street, an attractive woman screeched. The wind swirling up from the sidewalk was blowing her short skirt up over her hips. Underneath were only sheer pantyhose, leaving nothing to the imagination. A passing man whistled admiringly. The woman's date, a burly youth with an irritated expression, punched the whistler through a restaurant's plate-glass window.

The wind howled.

The police threw their prowl car into gear, abandoning Sarah as they screeched a tight U-turn across the street.

Inside the restaurant, several angry patrons had joined in the brawl. It was beginning to look like Barfights Of The Rich And Famous. The cops jumped from the car and tried to interfere. One of them got slugged for his troubles, so he brought out his sidehandle baton. The cops waded into the mêlée, clubbing everything in sight. It didn't help things much.

And over it all, the devil wind laughed.

I dropped the chunk of brick back into a planter as Sarah swaggered toward me. "Hey, was I quick or what?"

"You should have been paying more attention," I grumbled. "Next time you may not be so lucky."

"Luck!? I had them *snowed*!"

"Temporarily. But they were still suspicious. They would have kept an eye on you, if only to make sure you weren't hooking. When your imaginary 'sister' didn't show up, they'd have picked you up again."

"Would you have done anything?"

I didn't mention the brick. "The cops and I are enemies. But I like to think we're on the same side. I don't hassle them if I can help it. Besides, I'm not getting paid for this."

Sarah snorted, squinting at me through the hot wind. "You keep saying that. Why are you doing it, then?"

"Because I'm an idiot," I grumbled, leading the way up the street.

And really, it was probably the best explanation there was.

LINOLEUM, the sign said, in neon block letters three feet high. It was the only decoration the featureless concrete building sported. All that identified it as a nightclub was the line of trendoid hopefuls waiting outside the entrance. An aloof-looking muscleman in a jumpsuit blocked the doorway, admitting only those whom he felt were an asset to the ambiance. It wasn't a muster I felt particularly hopeful of passing. "Think we'll get in?"

Sarah gave the huddled line the contemptuous look that pretty teenage girls seem to master at an early age. She adjusted the silver belt, raising the shirt's lower hem until it barely concealed her panties, if she was wearing any, which I wasn't entirely sure about. "We'll get in."

I looked at about two yards of tanned, slender, sixteen-year-old leg, and realized she might just be right.

The wind whirled around the club like a dervish as we approached. A passing car tossed out a cigarette, red sparks flying. The wind caught these, swirling them in a devil's dance around the club's entrance before they finally died.

Despite the heat, I felt the back of my neck grow cold.

As Sarah had predicted, we had no trouble getting in. When her lithe, tanned, teenage self pranced up along the sidewalk, the muscular doorman almost swallowed his gum. Elbowing a couple of faded starlets aside, he elegantly opened the door. Only a twinge of warning in his voice marred the welcome.

"Eighteen and older . . ."

"Don't worry about it," I growled, stepping up behind her. The doorman looked at me in sudden hostility. "Who—?"

"Klaus is my bodyguard," Sarah tittered. "Daddy says I have to take him everywhere now that I'm legal."

I slipped the doorman some green in a bored manner. He shrugged, the money vanishing. "Go on in."

The interior was a dark, noisy hallway. A hostess in her mid-twenties waited beside a small desk with a hand stamp. "Over twenty-one?"

"Yes," said Sarah.

"No, she's not," I broke in.

"Klaus!"

"Your father was quite explicit," I said. "So don't bother with the fake I.D."

"Poop." Sarah extended her right hand. "I only have a year to go."

"Two," I growled.

The hostess smiled tiredly. "Left hand, please." Sarah reluctantly extended her other hand and got it stamped. I forked over the fifty dollar admission and the hostess stamped my right hand without asking any other questions.

She gestured at a door behind her and I pulled it open. The noise quadrupled. Lights flashed. And vast quantities of people jumped around inside. I gave a small internal shrug as I followed Sarah in.

Whether Jason showed up or not, at least it was out of the wind.

14

The music was live and as wild as the night. A group of musicians lined a stage at the front of the room, playing noisy dance tunes with a frenzied vengeance. I eyed them amusedly. Not one of them would have been able to get past the doorman under normal circumstances, but they played pretty well.

Sarah tugged at my jacket. "They never checked my I.D.," she said delightedly, practically shouting over the music. "You're a pretty good actor."

"Just a good liar," I growled. "You see your damn boy-friend yet?"

"He's not my—"

"Shaddup. He around?"

Her face clouded as she looked around the club's interior. Besides the crowds of people, there wasn't much to see. The club's name was well-chosen. L.A. has its share of luxury night spots, but Linoleum was not one of them. This was one of those stark joints that seems to survive simply from being temporarily in vogue. The few tables were formica garage-sale rejects, the chairs scarce and rickety. The industrial-grade concrete walls were decorated with broken mirrors and spray-painted designer graffiti. Flashing lights and speakers hung from overhead cables. There was no air conditioning: just a score of ceiling-mounted Venturi vents that whirled frantically in the gusting wind outside.

It was hot, noisy and uncomfortable. And from Sarah's expression, I could tell that Jason was nowhere in sight.

"Not here, eh?"

"I don't see him—" Her voice took on a slight edge of desperation. "But I know some of the guys in the band.

We'll ask them." She pulled at my hand. "Come on, let's dance."

I was appalled. "No fucking way."

"Come on! We have to get over there anyway . . . haven't you ever danced before?"

Actually, I had. It was a long time ago, back in my early twenties. Alexander and Kathy L'Hiboux would often go out, dining, dancing, laughing and in love.

But those were times long gone, a life that died when the Owl was born. And I would not mock its memory now.

"You dance if you want. I walk."

"Ohhh . . . you're no fun." Sarah bipped ahead of me, swirling and prancing among the throngs. Interested young men whirled around her, caught my eye, and drifted away again like leaves before the wind. I just pushed quietly through the crowd in the little redhead's wake, trying to look like the club bouncer or something.

My skin prickled. The excitement of the dancers was wild, verging on hysteria; infected by the scent of the devil wind whirling through the ceiling vents. The band's beat pulsed and the air crackled.

And someone was calling Sarah's name.

Some ten feet away, I saw the little redhead react. A strikingly handsome young man with a model's face and smoldering blue eyes pushed his way through the crowd. Sarah's face was a sudden tumult of surprise and relief.

"Jason! Oh, thank God . . . "

So this was the long-sought Jason. I eyed him sourly through the crowd. Though my deep prejudice against dealers darkened my view, I had no difficulty in understanding why Sarah found him attractive. But it was more than looks. His eyes had that careful intensity of purpose that often denotes both drive and intelligence. Jason Magrina was the type of young man that intended to go places, do great things.

It was unfortunate that he'd started on the wrong side of the law.

I pushed through the dancing crowd. Jason had not yet seen me, taking Sarah hastily by the arm and pulling her towards a secluded corner of the room. Though I could not hear their voices, I saw Jason ask a brief, intent question. Sarah's face looked a little disappointed, but her hands gestured, explaining something. Jason's eyes grew angry. He asked something else. And I was close enough to hear Sarah's answer.

"The man who rescued me brought me." She extended a small hand in my direction as I stepped up beside her. "You've heard of the Owl?"

He had indeed, if the sudden paling of his features was any indication. But he recovered quickly, sticking out his hand.

"My God. Of all the people I never thought I'd ever speak to, much less thank. I came here to meet somebody else, I didn't expect—"

"Steve couldn't make it." His face registered surprise. I ignored it, ignoring his hand as well. My face was impassive. Up close, I could see that his skin had a pale, twitchy quality about it. He'd been on the run for a few days, and it showed. "I told Sarah I'd get her here. I did, so I'm done. I think you two have something to talk about."

Jason gave Sarah a quick glance in which caution and urgency were nicely mixed. "Yeah. I guess we—" He broke off, staring over the heads of the dancers. His height was close to mine. "Oh, Jesus."

I turned. The band had just finished a piece and the scattered applause was dying away. In the sudden silence, three men in dark, expensive suits had just stepped through the club's entrance, a gust of hot wind behind them. For the briefest instant, it wafted open the jacket of the tallest one, exposing the faint dull gleam of a Parkerized ·22 auto.

"Sandoval tribesman," came Jason's voice behind me. But I knew that already. I half-zipped the front of my battle jacket. Outside, through the ceiling vents, I could hear the wind chuckle.

"We better split up." Jason was keeping his head low, his eyes on the men surveying the room. He half-shoved Sarah toward me. "You stick with your guardian angel, babe. It's me they're after. See if you can distract 'em for a while. If I can make it to the main breakers I'll blow the lights and you can fade. You can meet me at Steve's tomorrow. I'll be there after three. Got it?"

"Jason!" But her words sounded in empty space. He was gone, sliding swiftly through the crowd like a cautious eel. The temptation to shoot the bastard was strong. But I fought it down. His plan was good – as far as it went. He wouldn't have known just how much hatred the Sandovals had recently developed for Sarah and myself.

"What are we going to do?" Sarah was pressing close against me. The Sandoval thugs were fanning out professionally, searching the room. I frowned.

"They want you alive – and they want to grab you quietly. So let's make that real difficult." I shoved her along toward the stage, where the band was just coming back on for another set. "You said you know the band. Think they'll let you sing?"

"I've practiced with them, yeah, but—"

"Like your boyfriend said. Distraction." I lifted her up on stage and sank back into the crowd. The band members reacted in surprise.

"Wait!" Sarah turned for a brief moment, bending down towards me with a scared face. Two of the Sandoval thugs had already spotted her, though I was out of sight. "What are you going to do about them?"

My smile was gently reassuring. "I'm going to kill them," I said.

15

I faded backward into the crowd surrounding the stage, trying to look in four directions at once. It should have been five. I immediately bumped into a harried-looking cocktail waitress. She blocked my path professionally. "Can I get you something to drink?"

Anything to make her go away. "Bloody Mary, but made with bourbon," I said. She nodded, jotting it down, and I was free to keep moving.

Up on the stage, Sarah was holding a brief, intent conversation with the band members. The lead guitarist shrugged and grinned. Looked like a go – a good thing. Two of the Sandoval thugs were drifting toward the stage with deceptive casualness.

The third had moved toward the back of the room, keeping an eye on things. I kept behind a group of tall partyers, circling the room to come up fast from behind.

Up on the stage, the lead guitarist shuffled toward the mike. "You ready to dance?" His voice was a reverberating boom. The crowd answered with an appreciative roar.

"A friend of ours is going to be joining us on this next number," the guitarist continued. "Ladies and gentlemen: Scarlet Serenade!"

The crowd, infected with the excitement of the evening and the wind, clapped enthusiastically as Sarah took the mike. She was certainly attractive enough to warrant the applause. Her slim tanned legs glowed in the stage light and the scarlet mop of hair was like a fiery nimbus around her elfin features. The whole place was watching her.

I moved carefully behind the first torpedo, keeping against the back wall. He was still scanning the room, but most of his attention was on the stage. Sarah's voice echoed melodiously from the speaker system.

"Thank you." She paused for the clapping to die down. Faintly, through the fans, I could hear the wind's intensity increasing outside. "I'd like to dedicate this song to someone very special." Her voice held a touch of strain, of sadness. Her eyes quested the room.

"*A song for Jason, wherever he is,*" I thought. "*Let's see what the son of a bitch rates.*" I kept moving toward the torpedo's back. Sarah's voice echoed quietly.

"It's called *Walk The Night*," she said, and the band crashed into the opening chords.

Even as the thug's neck snapped under my fingers, I suddenly realized she was singing to *me*.

A city of lights, all darkness to me
The fire is within, burns too bright to see
I'm living in pain,
I just want the truth
'Cause I can't sleep at night

I eased the dead assassin to a seated position at an empty table, slumping him forward as though he'd passed out. Nobody noticed. All eyes were on the front of the room.

My love that was once a part of my life
Has vanished in blood, in pain and in strife,
I walk through the streets
So empty and still
And I can't sleep at night

Damn. I'd heard the song before – it was a fairly popular tune at the moment – but Sarah was changing some of the words. And, God help me, she could really *sing*. Her voice was a melodious contralto, speaking right to the libido. Despite the lyrics, couples were swinging into slow, pelvis-grinding dances. Up on the stage, Sarah's head was back, her eyes closed, giving it everything she had.

> *Though I walk*
> *Like a living man*
> *Death's chilling scythe*
> *Is within my hand*
>
> *And though hell's flame*
> *Burns inside my soul*
> *My eyes are stone*
> *And my gaze is cold*

Even the remaining two Sandoval thugs were fascinated. Both were close to the stage now, about ten feet apart. Dancers gyrated slowly past them, but the assassins paid no attention. Sarah was theirs as soon as she left the stage.

"Here you go." The waitress was back, bearing a blood-red drink. I gave her a ten, and waved away the change. She vanished in the crowd as I sipped the concoction, feeling the bourbon burn as my teeth stained red. I put the drink on a table and moved forward, masked by the crowd.

My right hand touched my left wrist and slid forth glistening steel.

> *Dreamers we once were, dreams we adored*
> *Now you're dreaming on and I dream no more*
> *I'm facing a life*
> *Without any rest*
> *'Cause I can't sleep at night*

The song was beginning to bother me. By chance or by design, the words hit too close to home. I shrugged it off, concentrating on the two torpedos. In the crowd, taking them out quietly was going to be tricky. Jason had apparently not found the main breaker yet – assuming he was even trying. I continued to ease forward. There was no other choice.

The wind blows red hot blood of the moon
I walk through the night, soul screaming for you
I'm living in pain
I just want the truth
'Cause I can't sleep at night!

Sarah's voice hit the last note and held it, lifting it like the wind outside. And I stepped forward, clapping the nearest assassin cheerfully on the shoulder. Even as he spun, surprised, I surreptitiously slipped four inches of razor-sharp steel through his second and third ribs. The end of the knife kicked in my hand as his heart jerked to a stop. He was dead standing up.

His buddy had seen me though, whirling in anger and reaching for his gun. I had anticipated that, my right hand drawing the dead assassin's own silenced ·22 before he even started to fall. Still keeping the body upright with my knife hand, I shot the other thug right out the back of the dead man's jacket, the *spit!* of the slugs inaudible over the music's end chords. The assassin staggered and sat down hard, as though he'd been jostled. My gun hand had never left the inside of the other thug's jacket. All eyes were still on Sarah.

She cut off the last note with crisp precision, her eyes still closed. The band slammed to a finish. The thug on the floor slumped quietly forward, eyes vacant and staring. The dead man on my knife fell backward, leaving red-stained steel in my hand.

Sarah's eyes opened, focused on me.

And all the lights went out.

Well, God damn. Jason had come through after all.

There was a good bit of noise from the crowd, mostly surprised exclamations and some laughter. No one had started screaming yet, though it probably wouldn't be long. I reached up toward the stage and found Sarah was already moving toward me. Swinging her off the stage, I kept my left arm around her shoulders as we pushed for the exit.

The crowd began to get a bit more unruly. Back toward the stage, I heard the *thump-bump* of somebody tripping over a dead body on the floor. There was a moment's pause. And then the screaming started.

I shoved for the door, guided by instinct and the faint orangish moonlight coming down through the vents. We were jostled and bumped, the screaming starting to come from all over the room. Panic is contagious in the dark, and the Santa Ana made it worse.

We burst from the club riding a wave of humanity, spilling out into the wind like a trendy tidal wave. My eye caught glimpse of a dark car across the street, seeming to contain several suits. Sandoval backup, naturally. Luckily, the wind had kept them inside the car. We stayed within the surging crowd, stampeding outward along the sidewalk. I kept my head down and my body in front of Sarah's. By the time the crowd thinned out, calming, we were already around the corner.

Only the wind followed us into the night.

16

We ended up on the roof of a West L.A. 7–eleven, taking shelter from the hot wind behind an air conditioning unit. Though it was almost midnight, the temperature was still well into the eighties. Perhaps it would have been gentlemanly for me to offer Sarah my jacket as a blanket, but she didn't need it and I did. I sat quietly beside her as she curled up sleepily on the warm asphalt roof.

"Owl?"

"What."

"Thank you for not abandoning me. I was afraid you were going to. You kept your end of the bargain."

The thought had occurred to me, too. On the other hand . . . "Your boyfriend vanished. And there were Sandoval thugs outside."

"I'm still glad."

I grunted. The wind blew spectral clouds of dust past the stars overhead. Sarah studied me quietly in the darkness.

"You really don't sleep, do you?"

"No."

"Not ever?"

"Not for nine years."

A quiet beat. Then: "What happened nine years ago?"

Fire. Screaming, burning; a thunderous explosion that woke me from the last sleep of my life. And Kathy's burned, mutilated neck under my fingers, her screams stopping as my eyes went blind with tears . . .

"Somebody tried to kill me. But I was asleep. They got my wife instead. Blew her apart, but she was still alive – what was left of her." My voice was a whisper, the pain was a tearing dagger in my mind. It had left a wound that

100

had never healed; and had sent me into the night forever. "She was . . . screaming. I had to . . . finish it."

Sarah's eyes were wide with shock. "Oh, God." There was a long silence as I stared straight ahead, not looking at her. Then she spoke again. "Did they ever find . . . ?"

I shook my head. "I found him myself. My own brother." I turned slightly, looking at her with my face as tight as a skull. "I'd been investigating a drug ring. Turned out he ran it. As you might guess, I'm not real fond of drug dealers."

She got the implication. "Jason's not like that!"

"Let's hope not." I went back to looking at the stars. The wind sighed around the air conditioner unit, the wafting dust almost a tangible wall outside our sheltered space. Sarah shifted slightly, the pebbly asphalt scrunching. I could feel her eyes still on me.

"Anyway . . . you haven't slept since?"

I shook my head. "Blessedly." *A nightmare to last a lifetime*.

A diffident pause, And then, almost inaudibly: "I wish I could quit myself. I keep seeing my dad . . . "

I felt suddenly ashamed of myself. In the tumult of dead bodies recently, I'd almost forgotten that this girl had lost her parents only the day before. The frantic pace we had been keeping had prevented her from dwelling on it, but in these quieter moments . . . nights could be rough. I stretched out a clumsy hand. "Yeah. I'm sorry . . . "

She took the hand gratefully, her slim fingers soft against the ridged scars and roughened skin of my own palm. A small, neat nail traced the ridge of callous running across the ball of my index finger, a mark of my profession. "I just try not to think about it." Her voice was still very quiet. She brought my hand to her cheek, resting against it wordlessly for a long moment as she stared into the wind. "I . . . I didn't like my mom much. I feel bad . . . even thinking that now, but it's true. We fought a lot. B-but . . . I *really* miss my *dad* . . . " She started crying. Silent crying, the deepest kind. Tears streamed in torrents from her eyes, pouring down in warm rivers over my hand; her face a wet, silent mask of misery. I looked at her in helpless despair, not knowing what to do . . .

She reached toward me and I took her, bringing her into my lap in a kittenish ball. She curled there for a long time, a shuddering, redheaded child in my arms. I watched the wind whirl in the night sky, feeling out of my element.

Finally, the shudders slowed and she stirred, groping at me. Her small face, still tear-streaked, pushed up next to mine.

"Make love to me?" The voice was small, needful, and earnestly imploring. I shook my head, lifting her in my arms.

"I can't do that, Sarah." Swinging slowly around on my knees, I lowered her back to her sheltered bed on the asphalt roof. I tried to keep my voice fatherly, which wasn't hard. For some reason, it was the way I was feeling at the moment. "You're just a little girl, and you need rest. Go to sleep. I'll still be here in the morning. And no one's going to hurt you while I'm around."

"Mmmph." Eyes closed, she shifted poutingly against the pebbly roof, getting into a more comfortable position. "Okay." There was a long pause, and then Sarah murmured again, sleepily.

"Owl?"

"Stop calling me that."

"There wasn't really a spider."

I blinked, saying nothing for a long moment, watching the orange three-quarter moon dance through the wind-whipped sky. "Then what . . . ?"

Her voice was a sleepy murmur. "I was afraid you'd really leave me at the club." She paused. And then, faintly: "Besides, like you said . . . you weren't getting paid."

I just sat, looking at the distant lights of the city. I'd stick with guns and knives. Young women were too hard to fight.

17

The wind sighed and Sarah slept at last. She'd be safe enough here; we'd climbed up unobserved. No one probably came up here for months at a time. As long as I was back before daybreak, she'd never know I was gone.

I stood, feeling the heavy reassurance of the twin shoulder holsters under my jacket. To Hell with the case. The Owl had been threatened. No matter what the reason, I had to do something about that. To have a price on my head put me on a mortal level. I had a reputation to uphold.

Catching a cab at that hour was difficult, but there was no other choice. Most of the bus lines had stopped running hours ago. To save time, I simply called the cab company from a pay phone, pretending to be a stranded motorist. In less than ten minutes, I was on my way to Beverly Hills.

But I was hardly travelling in luxury. The best cabs don't work late nights in Los Angeles – not enough business. This vehicle had no air conditioning and a driver whom I suspected was a recent escapee from Camarillo State Hospital. An emaciated black man in his mid-twenties, he had the radio blaring from both front and rear speakers and was pounding the wheel wildly even while he drove. All the windows were open, and the Santa Ana was howling through the cab unimpeded.

"Fuck the wind! Fuck the wind! Fuck, fuck, fuck the wind!" The driver chanted this over and over in time to the rap music on the radio, pounding on the wheel the while. It was a sentiment I shared, but his enthusiasm seemed excessive. And the speakers were painfully loud. I leaned forward.

"Hey, buddy – you want to kill these rear speakers, or you want me to do it for you?"

He reacted in anger, turning almost completely around in his seat, though the cab continued to speed down Sunset. His teeth were a rotten snarl, his eyes wide but the pupils far too small. Damn, a speed freak. "Whatchusay, mutherfucker?"

I smiled nastily and plunged Elvira's blade through the speaker grill to my right, then ripped it sideways and out again. Wires sparked as speaker cone shredded, and the sound from that source stopped dead. It was still plenty loud though. I never took my eyes from the driver's.

"Next cut goes in your face," I told him sincerely. He checked my size and decided to believe. Swearing incoherently under his breath, he lunged back to the radio and switched off the rear speakers, but turned the volume up on the front ones. Spite. I ignored it and he angrily ignored me. We drove on through the wind, and I spent the time surreptitiously digging the magnet out of the damaged speaker to my right.

The cab left me off on Palm, the driver cursing me even as I handed him a $20 tip. I'd expected that, so I took it back at gunpoint. No way he'd call the police, as blatantly buzzed as he was. Still swearing at me, he yanked a pipe and a crystal of what look like rock candy from the glove compartment, lighting up as he screeched away. Crystal methedrine "ice". Not too common, but growing in popularity. I shook my head and started north.

Sneakers carried me the final two blocks to Maple. There was no problem finding the Sandoval mansion. It had been in the news often enough. A stately Colonial-style dwelling the size of a major hotel, it had an ironic resemblance to the White House. The pillared and colonaded exterior was faintly visible in the moonlit distance, half-obscured by wind-tossed trees. It was a mere hundred-yard stroll from the road. Easy as pie. The only things in my way were alarm systems, security cameras, armed guards, and a twelve-foot iron fence. The wind's hot breath was a warning premonition of doom – a warning which I scarcely needed.

Ignoring the main gate, I circled instead to the downwind side of the lot. The main entrance would be where most of the security was located, in case of a full-scale assault by law enforcement agencies. The rest of the landscape would be dotted with security gizmos, but I had an edge.

I had the wind.

A howling Santa Ana plays hell with monitor systems. Motion detectors go nuts, what with windblown debris and foliage. The only thing to do is turn them off, before your security system overloads with false readings.

Infra-red cameras are designed to spot hot humans against cold landscape. But when that landscape has been baking in hundred-degree heat for two days, and is still almost ninety degrees in the hot wind . . . an armored Owl is almost invisible.

I came up on the downwind fence at a low rush. I didn't know if there were dogs, but I doubted it. Dogs grow irritable in the gritty wind, tending to fight. Chances are they were kennelled, but the wind would blow my scent away in any case. The fence itself was a problem, though. The high iron bars would not be difficult to climb, but the fence itself was probably hooked to an induction detector. A large chunk of meat such as myself would register at a touch. And if the half-burnt rabbit carcass I saw decomposing beside the lower railing was any indication, the next response would be a friendly welcome of 20,000 volts.

From the cover of a scrubby mass of foliage, I surveyed the fence carefully. Security cameras mounted on poles set well inside the border swung slowly back and forth. They were equipped with Starlyte lenses, able to see clearly even at night. The trees were all trimmed to prevent any branches from overhanging the fence. And there were no doubt plenty of pressure pads buried under the dirt on the other side, set to detect the weight of an intruder.

Tricky. But the wind came to my aid again.

One of the trees, an ancient, spreading willow, was swaying ponderously in the hot wind. Though its branches had been trimmed, the gardeners had not taken wind into account. And this night was *very* windy. The slender, supple willow branches, pliable as a whip and almost as strong, were stretching their ends a good five feet over the top of the fence when the wind blew hard enough.

It was all I needed. Now the only trick was timing.

It took a bit of waiting, but finally, the pole-mounted security camera was swinging away from the tree's area just as a powerful gust of desert wind flung the stretching green arms of the tree over the barrier. I was running before I realized it, reflexes triggered by instinct rather than by conscious thought. I only hoped I had guessed the defenses correctly.

I hit the fence with both feet, impacting the iron bars with rubber-soled shoes, at the same time hurtling upward to grab a double fistful of green branches. A yank and a leap, and I was near the top of the fence.

Then the wind died suddenly. The massive tree swung back, the puny two hundred pounds of Owl barely a noticeable hindrance. I shot over the top of the iron spikes as though hurled by a slingshot. Like Tarzan, I sailed through the air, clinging to the greenery still in my fist.

I let go at the peak of my arc, spinning in the wind to take the whipping branches against my Kevlar-armored back. I rattled through the tree's outlying fronds, bounced painfully from a larger branch, then landed on my ass with a *thud*. The jar practically knocked my fillings loose, but I was a good fifteen feet inside the fence. Well beyond any likely sensor pads. And the cameras hadn't seen a thing.

A good thing, too, I mused, rubbing my butt painfully. To have such an uncool entrance captured on video would have done the Owl's rep as a dangerous dude no good whatsoever. I adjusted my jeans and looked around for other monitors.

There was one, fixed high in a tree and about thirty yards away. Easy to avoid. The remaining monitors were mounted at various places around the eaves of the house. I would deal with those when the time came. About all that was left to worry about were pressure sensors. They could be anywhere. But they probably weren't.

If someone were sneaking up on the house, he would probably dodge from tree to tree. A casual stroller, such as Enrique himself after a heavy meal, would most likely stick to the paths. In the interests of economy and accuracy, therefore, the pressure sensors would most likely be buried near trees and other cover. Therefore, I squared my shoulders, lifted my chin, and made boldly straight for the house.

On my belly. I wasn't going to be an idiot – I might be wrong. And crawling kept my weight distributed widely. The sensors were probably set at eighty pounds, to avoid registering dogs or other animals. I'd have no more than twenty in any one area.

It was hardly glamorous, though. The wind blew dust and leaves in my face, and my belt buckle scraped dirt up like a plow, dumping it inside my jeans. That was tolerable until I crawled over an anthill without realizing it. Then the night just got miserable. I took some time out for slapping and cursing, glad only that the wind kept either from being audible. I finished off with some well-placed scratching, studying the remaining fifty feet to the house as I did so.

Fortunately, the really high-placed druglords have a strong and rather justifiable sense of their own invulnerability. They have so many cops, judges and city officials in their pockets that they usually know about a raid even before the chief of police. Their business competitors rarely strike without plenty of advance hostility. And any petty criminal or professional burglar has too much sense to mess with an edifice housing such dangerous inhabitants. A man's home is his castle; but in Enrique's case, it was a fortress.

However, the Owl was an anomaly. I was a pissed-off renegade with my reputation at stake and nothing to lose but my life. In my business, that was an even trade.

I was near the rear corner of the mansion, a darkened section three stories high. A single monitor overlooked the area, mounted high on the roofline under the sheltering branches of an immense oak. The tree was a security risk, obviously, but aesthetics had ruled in its favor. It framed the mansion nicely, and allowed moonlight to dapple a rear patio. Besides, none of the branches near the house were large enough to support a man's weight.

But I wasn't planning on climbing. I just needed that camera out of the way, and I needed to do it in a manner that would not arouse suspicion. Drawing the Waster from my right shoulder holster, I took careful aim and fired.

Speee! The shot went wild, blown off course by the wind. It careened from a rooftile and vanished, spinning end-over-end. I swore, then aimed again, waiting for a lull.

Spak! That was more like it. The pellet snicked through a leafy branchlet, causing it to snap in the wind. The green bark and wood prevented it from breaking away completely, however. It just folded downward limply – and the massy wad of leaves and green acorns were right in front of the monitor's lens.

I could imagine the annoyance of the mansion's security. A branch snapped. One more wind-related problem. But there was no way they would send someone out on that dark roof during a high wind. Fixing it would have to wait.

I stood up from the bushes, brushed dirt and insects from my clothing, and strolled toward the house.

Peering carefully through darkened windows, I finally found one that looked like a minor office; probably a secretary's warren and not likely to be used until morning. The window was alarmed, of course, but nothing fancy. I slipped Elvira from her sheath, running the flat of the steel blade along the sill until it suddenly tugged in my hand. the magnet was imbedded in the window here, the reed switch in the frame below. I jammed the knife between the two, and took the magnet I had stolen from the cab speaker from my pocket. Letting it stick to the knife magnetized the entire blade. The reed switch would stay closed now even if the window was opened.

A small, diamond-tipped glass cutter is part of the Owl's standard equipment. I sliced a neat circle in the window, undid the latch, and slid it open.

There wasn't a sound.

Inside, I swung the knife around, closed the window and removed the blade. Back to normal, except for the small circle in the glass. Lowering the shade concealed that. I stepped across the small cubby and peered out. I wasn't worried about interior alarms or motion detectors. The house exterior had shown lights still on, movement inside. All I had to do now was avoid being spotted.

The cubby appeared to be one of several set off from a larger, almost circular study-cum-meeting room. A stout woman in an expensive maid's uniform was running a vacuum over the carpet. As I watched, she finished, unplugged the vacuum cleaner and took it into one of the other cubbys. I sidled out.

The maid had her back to me, rummaging in a file. From the back of it she produced a half-full bottle of decent Scotch, began twisting off the cap. She shoved the door closed with her heel. I headed for the far door as a faint rythmic gurgling sounded behind the expensive panelling.

Outside the main door was a vast foyer framed by an immense double staircase in white marble, straight out of an old MGM movie. At the base of the staircase two men stood talking, one in a dark suit, the other in a thick velour dressing gown. I had no idea who the suit was. But the thickest elderly man in the dressing gown was Enrique Sandoval.

I'd come in on the tail end of a conversation. The suit was saying something.

" . . . unfortunately, no. But we are closing in his associate. Taps and tracers are in place. We should have the bitch by tomorrow."

Sandoval's head nodded ponderously. "Good. Take care of it. And be thorough. This has gone on long enough."

The suit nodded briskly and started toward the front door. I pulled back slightly as he passed. Sounded to me like the Sandoval association had managed to track down the mysterious Steve somehow. If Sarah and I went there tomorrow, we would be walking into a deathtrap.

The suit opened the front door and went out. I heard the wind moan outside.

A quiet voice sounded from the top of the stairs. "Your bath is drawn, sir."

"All right." Sandoval ascended the marble stairs at a measured pace. Peering from the doorway again, I saw a tall, dignified butler-type escort the heavyset druglord down a side hallway.

No one else in sight. I slipped out the door and headed for the nearest staircase at a quiet run. I was just starting up when a doorway between the staircases opened and a man stepped out.

I pressed back against the wall, trying vainly to make myself invisible against the white marble. Damn house was active as hell, considering it was past midnight. I had drawn the Waster. Not quick enough for my taste, but the Peacemaker's roar would be decidedly unsuitable in what I was hoping to keep a clandestine operation.

Luckily, the guy didn't even look in my direction. He was dressed in one-piece tailored coveralls, like a Beverly Hills technician. I got a glimpse through the doorway he had exited before it shut. Video monitors and flashing lights. The room under the stairs was the security station.

The technician opened the door to a small bathroom off the foyer and shut the door. I let my breath out and moved swiftly up the stairs.

A brisk trot down the hallway revealed a number of doors, all shut but one. This was a massive two-door entry, set in its own alcove with miniature pillars. Tacky, but I was hardly the Fashion Police. One door was open invitingly, revealing an immense sleeping chamber with a king-size four-poster bed and ornately lavish furnishings. Through the gauzy curtains of the immense bay window, I could see the dark trees outside tossing in the hot wind. They were faintly distorted. Thick glass; bulletproof, naturally. I was glad I had chosen the entrance I had.

There was a smaller door set against one wall, from which I heard faint sounds of splashing. This was Enrique's room, all right. I went in fast and slid under the bed just as the butler emerged from the bathroom door.

He hadn't seen me. I eased further under the bed, feeling cramped and getting dust up my nose. You'd think a criminal multimillionaire druglord could at least get his bedroom properly vacuumed.

The butler turned down the covers neatly, then exited the room without a sound. From under the bed, I could hear Sandoval carolling a Central American folk song in the bathroom as he towelled off. For a murderous drug-pedalling scumbucket, his voice was surprisingly decent.

Soft footsteps sounded from the bedroom door. I shifted my gaze and groaned inwardly.

A girl stood timidly in the doorway, bosomy, dark, and frightened-looking. Maybe eighteen, certainly no older. The butler was standing beside her, his face impassive. He gestured into the room and the girl entered meekly. She was wearing only a lacy silk robe that barely concealed the newly-bloomed body beneath.

The butler shut the door, and from the bathroom, I heard Sandoval's deep voice. "Ah. Rosa. *Está bien?*"

His voice was gentle, reassuring . . . the old bastard. The girl nodded meekly. Sandoval moved ponderously toward the bed, continuing the conversation in Spanish, obviously enjoying the moment.

Under the bed, I gritted my teeth. From Sandoval's polite questions and the girl's monosyllabic replies, I was able to deduce that she and her family had wanted to flee El Salvador into America. Sandoval had graciously arranged for this to happen. Now she was in America, yes? And they would soon follow? Yes, and they are well, that is good. Rosa received her green card, yes? And a good job?

"*Si.*" The girl lifted her chin with proud resignation. Lifting the robe from her shoulders, she allowed it to drop to the floor. Her breasts were large and newly ripened, her hips still slim and youthful. But her face had become a woman's; deep with inner strength. A bargain had been struck, and the bargain would be kept. It was time to pay the price.

And there wasn't a damn thing I could do about it. If I killed the bastard now, the organization would never believe

111

that the girl was not involved. She would die, and probably her family as well. For her sake and theirs, I had to stay where I was.

Besides, I had need of Sandoval alive.

The porky druglord enjoyed the next few minutes a lot more than I did. His fat body made quite a dent in the mattress, and he moved around a lot. No matter where I squirmed, the plunging bed seemed determined to crush me against the floor. I felt sorry for the girl underneath him. He had a lovemaking technique like a rutting hippopotamus.

She didn't cry, though. As a matter of fact, she threw in some inexperienced-sounding moans of fake delight that she'd probably been advised of by friends. They worked, anyway; Sandoval grunted loudly in satisfaction and rolled off her, panting heavily. The whole thing had taken less than three minutes.

"Ah . . . !" he groaned. "Ahhhh. *Magnifico*. Now get out."

Classy dude.

The girl rolled from the bed, her legs a little unsteady but her chin still proud. She bent down to pick up her robe from the floor.

And saw me.

We both froze. Her dark eyes were wide, her mouth opening for a scream. All I could do was put a finger to my lips in a desperate gesture for silence.

It worked. She closed her mouth, the dark, pained-looking eyes flicking to the fat, sodden creature on the bed. And then suddenly, the hurt in her eyes was gone.

She smiled at me. Then she picked up her robe and put it on, moving toward the door. She gave me one last glance, then looked toward Sandoval.

"*Adiós*," she said to the man on the bed. And I could tell from her voice that she meant it.

18

The wind was a faint moan through Sandoval's window; a thin scratching of skeletal branches against the bulletproof windows. Sandoval had shut off the room lights from a bedside control, and the grunts and shifting in the bed above me had gradually subsided. It seemed like forever, but was probably only ten minutes later that the snores started. I eased myself out from under the bed.

The room was dark. Only a faint orange light from the setting moon gave any illumination and it was eerily broken and shifted about by the blowing trees outside. The wind moaned creepily. I nodded with satisfaction. It would do.

The corpulent druglord lay on his back amidst silk sheets, mouth open and chins sagging as he snored lustily. I drew the Peacemaker, stuck it in his mouth, and cocked the hammer with my thumb.

The clicking as the hammer went back wasn't loud, but criminal types react to it instantly. Sandoval's snores stopped with a choke and his eyes flew open.

"Hello, Enrique," I said softly.

His eyes widened further. In that dark room, he could barely see me, but what he saw was enough. I let my teeth flash in a deliberately unreassuring grin. "Just thought I'd drop in. You were *asleep*."

I gave the last word some emphasis, just in case he needed a clue. His lips trembled, but the Peacemaker's barrel was in the way. I eased it back slightly. He wasn't stupid enough to try anything. "L'Hiboux."

"That's right, Enrique." I had dusted off and straightened my clothes before waking him up, since I wanted to give the impression of dangerous ease. "Just popped in for a moment

113

to warn you about a couple bad habits you got. See, you keep letting your thugs piss me off, and that's bad enough. But on top of it all, you keep going to *sleep*." I shook my head in mocking sorrow. "You ought to know better than that, Enrique. One of these days you might never wake up." I grinned again over the cocked ·45. "Know what I mean?"

Sandoval's tongue licked his thick lips carefully, but his voice had a hint of bluster. "I hope for your sake you brought the Scarlotti girl."

Whunk! I jammed the Colt's barrel so deep into his throat he gagged, and I kept it there by leaning on it as I snarled down into his purpling face.

"You don't seem to be getting the point, Enrique. You're fucking with the *Owl*. The girl is under *my* protection and you've got a dozen dead bodies to prove it. Back off or there'll be more – and you will be one of them." I eased back on the gun, letting him breath again. My teeth shone in the darkness. "You really don't want me to come back, Enrique. Not for a mere six pounds of snow."

"Six p—" For a moment, Sandoval's purpled face had a startled expression. Then his lips flickered in a strange way. In the darkness, it might almost have been a smile; faint, mocking, and gone in an instant. He coughed, rubbing his throat painfully.

"By tomorrow, L'Hiboux, you will regret even knowing my name," he promised. "And you will bring that girl most willingly, I assure you."

"Another bauble for your tiny prick, I suppose," I sneered. "You'll be dead before that happens."

"Hollow threats." His eyes mocked me. "If you are going to kill me, why not do it now?"

I sank two fingers deep into the sagging flesh of his throat, pinching off the carotid artery that supplies blood to the brain. I leaned over him as his eyes glazed, making sure that my face would be the last thing he remembered.

"Because I want you to suffer first, you piece of slime," I told him. And the edge in my voice rang true.

He went limp under my fingers. I backed away carefully, lowering the Peacemaker's hammer. Ten minutes, more or less, until he came to.

The bedroom door opened. And a knife gleamed in the darkness.

I leaped. *Thak!* The Peacemaker's barrel slammed down on a wrist, the big butcher knife spinning free and thudding to the carpet. There was an audible gasp, which I silenced by yanking the knifeholder into the room and against the wall. She was warm and fragrant and struggled like a demon.

"What the Hell are you *doing*?" I hissed, keeping a hand over her mouth. She bit my finger and I pulled the hand away quickly.

"You did not kill him!" Her voice was a furious hiss. "I listen outside the door. I have my knife. I finish the job you do not have the *cojones* to do!"

"Don't be stupid—"

"I knew I would do this. From the moment I met him. I pay the price for my freedom, yes. But now he must pay mine!"

I held her back against the wall. "They'll kill you. You, and your family, too. Don't be stupid. Let me handle it."

"*You*? He is there, yet you did not—"

"Rosa!" My hand was over her mouth again. The brown eyes flashed in the night. "Get out of here. Live your life. He will die, I promise you. And soon."

Over my hand, the snapping eyes remained stubborn. I bent and picked up the gleaming steel blade from the carpet, holding it out. "And the way he dies will be most satisfying. Even to you."

A gleam of orange moonlight glanced from the blade and flickered over the hard outlines of my face. She looked at me – and believed. The anger in her eyes subsided.

"You are *El Tecolote*?" she asked, her voice a whisper.

I nodded. She straightened then, taking the knife and tucking it away in her robe. "I hear of you," she said, quietly. "Please do not fail me."

I opened the door to the hallway carefully. No one about. On the bed, Sandoval was still out cold.

"I won't," I said.

I hoped.

She moved away down the corridor, a proud dark outline in a hallway corruption had bought. The wind noise was louder here, the mansion now dark and silent. She pushed open the door to a smaller bedroom, looked back, then vanished inside.

I took a deep breath. 3:30 a.m. It was time to go.

I hit the stairs at a silent rush, descending fast while keeping an eye out for hostiles. Sandoval wouldn't be out for long, and when he woke up, all Hell would break loose in here. Getting back out through the defenses would take an annoying amount of time; time I wasn't sure I had.

But there was another way.

I turned left at the base of the stairs, drawing the Peacemaker as I did so. No pause for planning – I had to move fast, and by instinct alone.

I went in through the door of the security room like a rocket, the pistol in my hand already swinging. Two technicians occupied the narrow room, admiring a *Penthouse* magazine. They jerked around, startled, even as the heavy Colt crashed down on the skull of the nearest. He slumped over the equipment as the other leaped up, drawing breath to yell. I swung a foot into his nuts. He let the breath out again in a barely audible whistle, his face whitening. I clubbed him with the Peacemaker's butt and he ended up face-down on the floor.

Three seconds or less, and they were both still alive, though unconscious. I let them stay that way. They were just technicians, not assassins. I reached over to the console, clicking off the various security units. I was pleased to see the rear video monitor still obscured by the branch, but the smugness was quickly counterbalanced by the discovery of several pitfall traps shown in a wall-mounted security map. From the looks of things, I had narrowly escaped tumbling into one. Sheer luck. But I knew where they were now. I left the security room at a silent trot.

The wind greeted me as I pushed the study window open again, the alarms now silent. I swung a leg outside, then paused. What the hell. Perched on the windowsill, I reached over to the nearby desk and picked up a phone, dialling the number from memory.

"Beverly Glen Limos?" I said. "Pick me up at the corner of Palm and Elevado in five minutes. Yeah, cash. I'll be waiting."

Distantly, through the thick walls, I could hear the sound of shouts coming from the upstairs bedroom. An angry voice, dazed. There was a crash as something was knocked over.

I grinned and hung up the phone. Slipping out the window, I walked casually away into the night.

WEDNESDAY

19

The faint red glow of the rising sun was just starting to color the windswept distance when the limo dropped me off, a couple blocks from the 7–eleven. The store itself was still closed, so I stopped in at an all-night donut shop to pick up some breakfast.

The Pakistani owner was behind the counter, packing a dozen chocolate-laden cholesterol bombs into a box. A haggard-looking truck driver waited by the register. "Gimme five Kwik-Piks, too," he said, tossing a bill onto the counter. "And make sure they're lucky ones this time. You lost me thirty-eight million last week, Hadad."

"Hokay." The owner put the box on the counter and pushed some buttons on the Lottery machine mounted by the register. It chattered a moment as the truck driver looked over at me with red-rimmed eyes. I smiled casually.

"Been up all night too?"

"God damn wind," he muttered, running a hand through his thinning hair. "I can't never sleep when the Santa Ana blows. I can't stay home, 'cause I fight with the old lady. And the damn bars close at two. She likes donuts, though. Maybe she'll let me in the house."

"A dozen chocolate, mebbee she sit on your face with her most enormous bottom until you sleep good, eh?" The owner gave the trucker a nudge. Obviously a steady customer. The trucker showed a wind-irritated flash of annoyance, but laughed in a strained manner.

"Wouldn't hear the damned Santa Ana, that's for sure," he admitted. Taking his ticket and the donuts, he pushed out the door into his enemy's embrace. It banged the door shut behind him in triumph.

"His wife, her bottom is that of an elephant," the Pakistani owner confided to me, with obvious relish and approval. "Chocolate donuts for you?"

"Uh, no." I had some Jamaican ancestry mixed in with the Indian, and my butt was big enough. And I could imagine Sarah's reaction. "Just a couple plain ones. And coffee."

"Hokay." The owner started putting donuts in a bag, and I glanced over at the morning *Times* sitting on the counter. It was certainly a violence-strewn page. Magrina's destroyed house, the shootout in the bank building, and the three dead thugs in the nightclub all had their own writeups. As yet, they weren't officially connected. But there was one murder I didn't recognize. STUDIO CITY GIRL SLAIN the headline read. It was down toward the center of the folded page, and that was all I could see. I flipped the paper open, and the photo of a pretty blonde about Sarah's age looked back at me.

"Allegra Simmons," it was captioned. Her parents had come home from work Monday to find her dead in her bedroom. She'd been tortured first.

I crumpled the paper in my fist. Damned Enrique. I should have cut his eyes out when I had the chance.

Shimming back up the locked ladder to the 7–eleven roof, I held the bag of donuts in my teeth as I peered cautiously over the edge. Sarah was still there, curled in a ball against the air-conditioning unit, looking like a stray kitten in the faint red light of dawn. She stirred as I approached, the pebbly asphalt roof crunching underfoot.

"Mmmmm. What time is it?"

"Breakfast," I said. "Donuts and coffee. You drink coffee?"

Sarah sat up drowsily, rubbing sleep from her eyes. One cheek was imprinted with the mark of the pebbly roof. She yawned. "No, but I'm too starved to be picky. Give it."

I handed over a styrofoam cup, peeling the lid off. "Good girl. It's hot."

Sarah took it, sipped, made a face, then shrugged. "So's the wind. Won't it *ever* let up?" She began rummaging in the donut bag.

I squinted into the flying grit, letting the street-person's well developed sense of weather do some estimating. "Not today. As a matter of fact, it may get worse."

"Great. Hey, no chocolate?" She was visibly chagrined, glowering at a plain donut.

"I thought you weren't going to be picky. Besides, your butt's big enough."

"Oh, God, is it big?" She half-turned in the wind, trying to get a look at her tight little posterior. I sighed inwardly. It is a universal truth that all women secretly think their bottoms are too large. Men have their own insecurity, but it is less visible publicly. "No. I was just kidding. Eat your breakfast." I wanted to get some food in her.

She was doubtful but ravenous, finally gave in, dipping a donut in her coffee cup and shovelling it down. "How was the night?"

"Dull," I said.

"It must be weird not to sleep."

"Boring, mostly. But I'm afraid I have some bad news." I pulled the torn-out newspaper article from my pocket and extended it toward her. "I hope I'm wrong, but the name's not common . . . "

"Oh, *NO!*" Her voice was an aghast wail. She grabbed the paper away from me and stared at the picture, her face going white.

"It's your friend then?"

She nodded dumbly, rocking back in a dazed manner to thump her head against the air conditioner. She didn't seem to notice. "Oh, God . . . Allegra."

"Which explains why the Sandovals are after you. She must have suspected you were seeing her boyfriend. They . . . interrogated her pretty badly. She would have told. And when they didn't get Magrina using her . . . "

" . . . they came after me." she finished. She was still white. "But, oh, Jesus, Owl . . . her voice on the tape . . . "

I nodded somberly. "They were there even then. But she was dead before we even heard it. There was nothing you or I could have done."

"God, I can't *believe* this!" Her face was more than anguished, it was *scared*. Allegra's was a death she could identify with more than the others. It really hit home. Even pretty, popular teenage girls can die. She turned terrified eyes toward me. "Owl . . . I'm – they're going to *kill* me!"

"They want you alive – for a while," I said. "And they won't even get that. Not as long as I'm here. I told you that before, and I meant it." I grinned with dangerous reassurance. "I've got a reputation to protect."

Her smile was a wry admission. "And you've been living up to it so far, anyway. I just wish I could pay you."

We looked at each other for a long moment in windy silence, lips twitching as we both realized we were thinking the same thing. Finally, we both laughed shortly, Sarah flushing and looking down shyly.

"No more spiders," I said, reaching for her hand and helping her to her feet. "This old heart can't take it. But it's a memory I'll keep." I took the newspaper article back and pointed at the coffee still in her hand. "If you're done with that, we should get off this roof. The manager will be showing up soon."

She nodded, taking a last sip from the cup and swallowing painfully. She was still upset, sick with anguish and worry. Making a face, she tossed the cup aside. "I'm ready, I guess."

I caught the styrofoam cup as the wind blew it past me. "Ah-ah," I admonished. "Try not to litter." I stuffed it into the empty donut sack. Sarah gave me a strange look as she headed for the ladder down.

"I forgot. You're a good citizen."

"Right."

"Who kills people."

I shrugged as I swung a leg over the edge of the roof, sliding to the ground on the edge of the locked ladder. "One way or the other," I said, "I'm just taking out the garbage."

She slid down the ladder after me and I caught her at the bottom, keeping my eyes averted. The shirt she was wearing as a dress kept blowing up around her hips. "We'd better get you another pair of jeans before you start causing traffic accidents."

She readjusted the belt to help hold the shirt down. "Are we going to Steve's now?" Her voice was quiet.

"Do you know where it is?"

"No."

"Then why did Magrina . . . ?"

"You told him Steve couldn't make it to the club. He must have thought you knew the place."

Oops. She was right. A case of the Owl trying to be too clever. "Hm. Well, it might be for the best, anyway. I have a . . . feeling it might be dangerous."

"You think the Sandovals know where it is?"

It was going to be hard to explain this without letting her know that I was gone most of the night. "Well, I overheard . . . " I began.

And then froze. My guts started knotting.

I'd heard Sandoval's underling say: *"We are closing in on his associate. Taps and tracers are in place. We should have the bitch by tomorrow."*

At the time, I'd thought they were talking about Jason, the mysterious Steven and Sarah. But then I remembered Sandoval's last words: *"By tomorrow, L'Hiboux, you will regret even knowing my name. And you will bring that girl most willingly, I assure you."*

The bastards were after Danny.

Sarah reacted to the sudden ice in my face. "What?" she began, but I was already racing for a pay phone.

A quarter in the slot, and I punched buttons frantically. Nothing. Phone was out of order. I swore and leaped to the one beside it. This one responded. I dialed the number again.

A sleepy male voice answered. "Hello?"

"Harry!" My voice was a ragged snap. "This is Al. Is Danny there?"

"Whoa." I could feel him jerk awake. It was important to keep the house isolated – I would never have called unless it was a dire emergency. "Uh, no, Al . . . she left for the office about five minutes ago."

I swore again. "Car phone?"

"No . . . she's been thinking about one, but—"

I hung up. No way to reach her. And if my guess was correct, the Sandovals would be waiting for her at the office. Damn the criminal swine. I should have known – they were far more dangerous than the Feds. They had the money to hire the best computer hacks and phone jockeys available, and no need to worry about legality or warrants.

I was running. Running toward the rising sun, the hot desert wind howling into my face. Behind me, I could hear Sarah's feet trying to keep up, her voice calling pantingly after me, demanding explanation. I ignored her. Down the street from the still-closed 7–eleven was a decrepit bar catering to the alcoholic crowd. It opened at 6 a.m., five minutes from now. And in the lot, a thrashed-looking Hell's Angel was climbing unsteadily from his Harley.

Hulking, shaggy and hung-over as hell, the biker didn't notice our approach. He tugged at the bar's unyielding door for a second, squinted at a watch, then stumbled for the side alley, fumbling at his fly. He never knew what hit him.

Sarah looked down at the unconscious body amongst the garbage. "Jesus, Owl, was that a fair fight?"

"This is an emergency," I growled, shaking my numbed hand as I rapidly searched his pockets with the other. "Dammit, where's his keys?"

"They're in the bike still."

"Damn! Say so next time." I swung her aboard the bike, then clambered on myself. "Hang on!"

"Can you drive one of these?"

I kicked the starter. The big Harley blasted into life with a full-throated roar of drag pipes. "You better hope so!"

126

"What's the goddamn emergency!?" She had to shout over the roar of the engine. I slammed the bike into gear and sailed from the lot, leaping over the curb into the street. I yelled back, over my shoulder.

"My business partner's in trouble!"

"Business partner!?"

"My *wife*, goddammit!" I yelled. We thundered away into the wind.

We hit Crescent Heights doing sixty, blasted across the Sunset intersection against the light and gave the thundering Harley full throttle up Laurel Canyon as the faint sound of colliding cars faded behind us. Sarah's arms were a terrified vise across my chest. "Jesus, Owl! You're going to kill us!"

"Don't call me Owl!"

The traffic in the narrow two-lane pass was snarled with commuters, but the Harley could ride the centerline. Trees, wind and oncoming trucks whipped past us as we thundered up the winding hill at ninety, the bike's malevolent roar the only warning most commuters got before we flashed by them on the left. Behind me, I heard more collisions.

"My dress is blowing way up!"

"I can tell."

We went over the crest of the hill like a motocross, the bike sailing through the intersection without touching the ground. Sarah screamed, but she'd been doing that at five-second intervals since the ride started. We hit the downslope with a tooth-rattling jar and thundered toward the Valley below.

The office was in Woodland Hills. I knew what the address was, although curiously enough I had never been there. I hit the 101 onramp at eighty and let the Harley fly.

A siren sounded behind us. Damn. Always a cop around when you don't need one. I swerved the Harley in and out of the rush-hour traffic, risking a glance back.

Highway Patrol. The black and white Ford had swung over to the emergency lane and was roaring up fast. The bike could smoke him, but not in this traffic. I had to do too much weaving. I swung to the right.

"What are you *doing*!?" Sarah shrieked. "You can't pull *over* – he'll *arrest* you!"

I swerved through the line of traffic to the emergency lane and gave the bike full throttle. "Hold this down!"

"What!?"

"This grip! Keep it twisted!" I released the throttle, grabbed her right hand away from my chest, and slapped it onto the rubber grip, yanking her wrist down. The bike surged ahead. Behind us, the siren was screaming like a banshee.

"What are you going to *do*!?"

"Slow the pursuit!" Still steering with my left hand, I drew the Peacemaker with my right and swung it wide, over Sarah's billowing red mop. She shrieked—

BOOOM! The pistol kicked against my hand, and Sarah almost yanked us into the guardrail. I countered with my left and brought the bike back under wobbly, high speed control. Behind us, the CHP cruiser skidded, right tire blown out. It fishtailed into the guardrail, spun across the lane, was sideswiped by a Cadillac and ended up crumpling its nose against a support post. Cars screeched and swerved, traffic tying up nicely. I heard a few smashed fenders. Lots of property damage, hopefully no serious injuries. A quick glance back showed the cops already jumping from the wrecked car.

"They'll radio ahead!" yelled Sarah.

"Let 'em," I said. "We're getting off here."

Up ahead, the freeway was built on elevated landfill, a steep embankment on either side leading down to the surface streets. A flimsy metal guardrail and a dense growth of scrubby California brush kept drunks from sailing off the freeway and landing in someone's back yard. But they still tried. A hundred yards ahead, the guardrail was torn away and the seven-foot high brush smashed and flattened for about twenty yards. The car had been towed away. But the trail it had left was a perfect emergency offramp.

I wrenched the cycle hard over, bouncing over the asphalt rise at the road's edge and catapulting us down the slope. Sarah screamed. Brush crashed. And the Harley came to rest in a tangle of coyote bushes only a few feet from the street below, but completely out of sight.

I was bent half-over the handlebars, the breath half-knocked out of me but otherwise fine. Sarah was practically on my back. I grunted in a cool manner and rolled off the bike carefully.

"You okay?" I started to ease Sarah to her feet, but the little redhead bounced up cheerfully.

"Was that way ever a *blast*?" she declared. "Let's do it again!"

Teenagers. I turned without a word and started running down the slope, plowing through the tangled bushes. Every second counted, and we were still two blocks from the office.

Since we had left such a snarl of traffic behind, the only witnesses to our exit would have been in cars on the other side of the freeway, travelling the opposite way. The bike would be found, certainly, but not before we were long gone. Sarah followed my trail down and we hit the sidewalks of Canoga in good time.

Woodland Hills is not exactly the densely forested area its name implies. The only trees there now were put there recently and on purpose, by landscape designers. The place is mostly skyscrapers and upscale offices; the last place in the world anyone would expect to find the Owl's office. Which is precisely why it's there.

We pelted down the sidewalk at a dead sprint, the wind howling overhead and the skyscrapers standing stark against a streaming sky the color of a blood-smear.

A block ahead, I saw a familiar grey AMD customized Mercedes turn into an underground lot.

"Danny!" I yelled. But I was too far away, and the car's tinted windows were shut against the blowing grit. I redoubled my pace, leaving a gasping Sarah trailing behind on the sidewalk. The car vanished down into the parking depths below.

I hit the ramp on the fly and pounded down toward the guard gate on foot, ignoring the signs warning against pedestrian entry. The portly guard, sweaty and annoyed-looking in his shack, lunged forth to stop me.

"Hey! Hey, asshole—!"

He wasn't armed. I sank a left into his generous gut and a right to his jaw. He staggered against the shack, rebounded, and stumbled toward me again as some commuter rolling down the ramp in a Jag blew his horn at me. I had no time for this shit. I grabbed the porky guard and threw him across the Jag's hood with a thump. The guy inside started yelling about his paint.

Sarah, panting, sprinted down the ramp to join me. Together, we raced into the concrete depths of the garage.

Danny's car was parked just one level down, but Danny wasn't in it. There was no sign of violence. I grabbed Sarah's arm and dragged her toward the elevator.

"What floor?" she panted, as the door dinged open.

"I don't *know*," I swore, pounding the "Door Close" button. The parking elevator only went to the lobby level anyway.

"You don't know where your own *office* is!?"

"I've never *been* here, dammit! I just know the address!"

The elevator dinged open again and we rushed out into the lobby.

It was more of a courtyard. The interior space was an immense triangle, walled by three skyscrapers and roofed with glass, ten stories up. Trees stretched toward the inaccessible sky above, and birds twittered and splashed in the landscaped courtyard waterfall. A restaurant had commandeered the area, elegant tables scattered amidst the jungle greenery. Various suits could be seen there, having power breakfasts and smugly eying the gritty wind visible through the glass above.

"Christ. The *Owl* has an office in *Disneyland*?!"

"Camouflage. Now shaddup." I ran a finger swiftly over a large black-marble building directory mounted near the main elevators. And stopped at the white legend: DENTAL PAIN RESEARCH – SUITE 808. "Here it is."

"You're *kidding*. Why—"

I was already dragging her into an elevator. "Prevents visitors." I hit the "8" button and the doors started to close.

"Hold the door, please." A suit tried to push his way on. I planted a foot in his chest and sent him sprawling back out to the floor. The doors closed.

At least the sucker was fast. We whined up to the eighth floor at turbo speed and jerked to a stomach-lurching halt. I already had the Peacemaker in my hand as I lunged from the doors, pointing back at Sarah. "Stay back!"

And then a different voice. "Al?"

Blonde, beautiful and confused, she was twenty yards down the corridor, her key in an office door. "What are you—"

"Danny! Get away—"

CRASH! Too late. The bastards came plowing out of the opposite office, slamming into her and sending her hurtling through the doorway she'd been opening. Two of them went in practically on top of her. A third tried, but I blasted a 225 grain Silvertip through his skull and splattered his brains over the doorjamb. But then a fourth cut loose with an Uzi.

BRAKAKAKAKAKOW! A fusillade of 9mm slugs ripped across the corridor, slammed into my chest, and tore into a wall-mounted fire alarm switch. *BRRAAAAANG!* The alarm bells began to sound, but I ignored them. I hit the carpet rolling, as the machine-gun assassin fired again. *BRAKAKAKAOW!* Carpet shredded where I'd been. They'd come armed for serious trouble this time. And they would find it.

BOOOM! The Peacemaker kicked in my hand, punching a first-sized hole in the hood's belly. I swore. Fatal, but not instantly. I'd been rolling as I fired and my aim was off. The hood staggered backward down the corridor, screaming and bleeding, but still trying to get his gun up.

131

Behind him, I could hear screams and shouts welling up from below. The end of the corridor was a balcony, looking out into the courtyard from eight floors up. The hood, still staggering backward, brought his gun to bear. And the Peacemaker roared again.

BOOOM! Minus a good portion of his head, the hood's body backflipped over the railing, the Uzi hammering wildly in the spasming hands. Slugs smashed and shattered through the glassed roof above as the body tumbled eight floors to fall with a thunderous *SPLASH!* into the elegant fountain below. Suits yelled in horror and fear as glass rained down into the suddenly blood-filled waters . . .

And the wind swirled in and howled.

I was paying no attention, of course. I was crouched in the office doorway, Peacemaker extended toward the two assassins inside. One of them held Danny in a tight clutch, staying behind her body. The other was standing in a casually mocking manner, pointing a ·357 at me.

"Where's the redhead, L'Hiboux?" He had to half-shout over the noise of the fire alarms.

I didn't answer. Danny's eyes were big and worried, her hands clutching her purse anxiously. It reminded me of the situation in Sarah's house, just two days before. But this was very, very different.

"Give us the girl and you can have your bitch," the hood sneered. "Otherwise, she dies right now."

"Fat fucking chance," I said, and blew him away.

Even as his body flopped against the wall, the one holding Danny jerked his gun in my direction. That was all it took. I hit the floor.

"ARGK!" The hood suddenly went white as Danny jammed her elbow back hard into his solar plexus. Her other hand emerged from her purse as she spun around, a vicious little Sig-Sauer double-stack nine appearing in her dainty fist. The thug only had time to gape. *POWPOWPOWPOWPOW-POWPOWPOWPOWPOWPOWPOWPOW!* Danny punched thirteen hollowpoint slugs through his chest cavity in less than two seconds, fogging the room with a fine spray of gore. She ejected the empty magazine, slammed in a fresh and flicked the action closed again before his shredded body had even hit the floor.

"What the hell *is going ON*!?" she snarled at me. "You were never supposed to come here."

"Couldn't resist," I said, rolling to my feet. At the end of the corridor, the shouts from the lobby increased in volume over the alarm noise. Sarah had run to the railing. She looked back, frantic.

"Police are here!"

"Hell." I jumped out into the corridor, smashing the glass on a fire extinguisher box with my elbow. What the Hell, the alarms were already sounding. I yanked the heavy red cylinder from its mount and ran with it to the railing.

The wind howled and moaned through the shattered glass above, pouring the heat and cinders of desert reality into the artificial paradise below. The waterfall was running red, the birds had scattered, and the smug, suited patrons were now huddled in terrified groups near the exits.

At the main entrance, blue-uniformed figures were running in, looking up toward the railing as bystanders pointed. They would be up here in moments. Time for a delay.

With a powerful heave that was ripping agony to my injured left arm, I hurled the heavy metal fire extinguisher out into space. It soared out over the cultivated trees, the red cylinder tumbling, people shouting . . .

And the Peacemaker kicked in my hand.

BOOOM-KABAAAAAM! The half-inch slug ripped through the high-pressure tank and the whole thing went off like a bomb. Two pounds of caustic dry fire retardant chemicals were blasted into the air in a white thundercloud, swiftly filling the lobby with an eye-watering, nose-searing, milk-white haze. Cops and citizens all threw themselves to the ground and started coughing.

Good enough. I grabbed Sarah and hustled her back toward the office.

Danny was just shoving a couple of irridescent optical disks into her purse. "All the records," she shouted over the alarm.

"What about the systems?!" The office was a maze of computer equipment, mixed with a comfortable and stylish decor. I was momentarily sorry that I would never have time to appreciate it.

"Fuck 'em!" Danny's hand flipped a switch on a desk control, pressed two buttons at once. Sparks and smoke began flying out of everything in the room. "Was time to upgrade anyway! What the Hell, you're rich – let's get out of here!"

"Yeah, but separately!" I pushed the redhead toward Danny and began scribbling on a piece of paper. "Take Sarah! I'll meet you at Chaos tonight!"

Danny gave me a furious look, but was too professional to argue. She and the confused redhead vanished through the smoke while I stuck the paper on one of the fallen bodies.

"Sweet Dreams, Enrique" it read. Then I raced for the exits myself.

20

Getting out was fairly easy; the balconies at the corridor ends were connected by walkways going clear around the courtyard area. I merely ran to the next skyscraper, went up one floor to avoid suspicion, and took the elevator down. This building's alarm was not ringing, so there was merely confusion rather than panic. The cops hadn't covered all the exits yet. I walked out the front door and away into the wind.

I caught an RTD on Ventura and headed east, settling down on the vandalized vinyl for a long haul. The busses get busy when the Santa Ana blows. No one wants to walk, not even short distances. The seats were crowded, but silent. The wind's gusts tended to rock the bus in an uneasy fashion, and the howling was less than restive.

I mused. My crudely bandaged wounds were aching and sore, now that the adrenal rush of emergency was fading. I ignored them. Away from Sarah's pestering personality, I found my mind sinking into deep introspection. There were several curious quirks in the current case. But the one that bothered me most was: *Why?*

Why was it happening? At first it had made sense. Magrina had stolen or lost six pounds of coke belonging to a South American mobster, and he was going to pay. That was standard. Since he had vanished, the mobsters had gone after his girlfriend. She had given them Sarah's name, then died.

But that was where things started to break down.

Why were they still after Sarah? It seemed beyond reason. Mobsters are drug-dealing criminal scum, but they are also businessmen. I had taken out over a dozen of their assassins in the past three days, and what with police investigations, legal difficulties and the sudden shortage of manpower their costs must be astronomical. They would still want me dead, but why waste time with the girl? With her under the Owl's protection, it would have seemed easier just to pursue Magrina directly.   I got off the bus on Hollywood Boulevard and caught another headed downtown. The downtown busses were dirtier. The wind whistled through a broken window and stirred up the acrid smell of rancid piss from the worn flooring. I briefly wondered how Danny and Sarah were doing. It had been a dirty trick, sticking Danny with the babysitting job, but it had been necessary. The redhead would be safe enough in Danny's capable hands. She wouldn't have been where I was going.

I needed some answers. And there was only one place to get them.

I got off the bus just east of downtown and walked south, the windblown dust stinging my cheek and getting in under my glasses. I kept my hand on my gun. No bus route goes through this section of town. Legend says there had been a Mayan temple here once, a thousand years ago. A place of blood sacrifice. Los Angeles, founded from a mission a few miles away, had spread itself over the forgotten ruins – and where it touched, it died. The area is nothing but dry, burned-out and abandoned factories, littered with gutted cars. There's no traffic and the few people you see out in the open are usually dead. It's a place so instinctively avoided by the natives that most don't even realize it exists. A place of crime and evil, where the shadows are darker and the air itself hurts to breathe. Coming here is dangerous. Staying here is insane.

And Cutter's is right in the middle of it.

Halfway down a battered street with the signpost missing is a narrow alley. The alley has a hole in the brick wall, vaguely doorshaped. The hole is black within, no light visible, but the sounds and smells emanating from it are warning enough. *Stay out!*

I went in. This was Cutter's.

The blackness was no illusion. Cutter's is *dark* inside. What little daylight seeps into the alley seems to stop dead at the doorway, afraid to enter. Only the wind followed me in, grit swirling in the smoky, stench-filled dimness. Like the Owl, it belonged here. Because this is the closest thing to Hell on earth.

The darkness concealed the various tables, where nightmarish creatures that might once have been men sat, drinking and brooding. Cutter's is a place inhabited by the evil and the diseased. Felons, the criminally insane . . . and worse.

From under the single dim light at the bar, Norbert the dead bartender hailed me mockingly.

"Owl, *ese*. Sit down and have one on me. You been busy lately, eh?" He grinned, his scrawny, skeletal frame bouncing slightly behind the counter.

I stepped toward him, keeping my guard up. The wind puffed red dirt across the greasy surface of the bar. "You've been reading the papers."

"Word gets around. Jesus?"

"Yeah."

Norbert swung the jug of purple liquid up from under the bar, poured it into a chipped shotglass. I hefted the drink in my left hand. Purple Jesus was a Cutter's specialty. 200-proof grain alcohol and grape Kool-ade. Illegal, but that hardly mattered here. Like me, Cutter's had no license, no legal standing. And it never closed. It couldn't. The hole in the wall that served as an entrance had no door.

Norbert was actively flamboyant today, his thin, greenish-white hands moving constantly over the bar. I nodded to him over the top of the glass, looking through the half-inch hole in his forehead to the broken mirror behind. I could see my own eye looking back. "You seem excited today." I drained the glass fast and swallowed painfully, keeping my gun hand at the ready. The price on my head made me doubly cautious in here.

"It's the wind." Norbert's pale, bulbous eyes widened cheerfully, his nearly lipless grin showing horselike teeth.

He pointed to the scar-lined hole in his head. "Blows through here. Tickles my brain. I get off on it, man."

I shook my head. There was a rumor that Norbert had a pact with Satan. The superstitious lot at Cutters believed it unquestioningly. I wasn't so sure. People had survived bullet wounds to the brain before.

"You're the only one who does, then." I dropped the glass back to the counter, hissing around the fire in my throat. "Alcatraz?"

"You know where to find him, *ese*." Norbert jerked his head towards the distant stairs at the back of the room. Wind gusted through the doorway again and he turned his forehead to catch it. "Heeheeeheeheeee . . . "

He was doing it on purpose, needling me. Norbert enjoyed being the Owl's only failure. He'd attacked me once, years back.

And I'd made that hole in his head myself.

I turned, moving through the shadows toward the staircase. Dark figures shifted slightly aside as I passed. I didn't look at them. In Cutter's, a man's face was his own business.

The stairs, usually damp and moldy, were dry and cracking from the wind. The boards split and popped under my feet, creaking like dry bones against their rusted nails. There was a single door at the top. I didn't bother to knock.

Alcatraz stood at one of the windows, his back to me, facing east. The room had two windows, a wooden floor and a wooden chair. Period. Both windows were open, the Santa Ana howling through. Alcatraz was facing into it unflinchingly, the wind whirling over the granite ridges in his face.

"L'Hiboux," he rumbled. He hadn't turned around. It was a mere acknowledgement – Alcatraz never wasted words. Slowly, he turned around.

Black hair, black eyes. Face as weathered as the native sandstone, and just as hard. There was no telling his age. He might have been fifty, but there were plenty that claimed he was older.

A *lot* older. Alcatraz was a full-blooded Mayan. The last one alive.

No one knew his real name. They called him Alcatraz because it fit. He was hard, impenetrable, unchanging. And he knew *everything*. He moved through this world like an eerie force, manipulating, controlling. People would find their lives suddenly changed for good or evil, dependent upon some great inner plan of Alcatraz's. Like as not I was part of that plan even now. Certainly, he had been there on that Hollywood street when this had all begun. I hated the feeling. But I had no choice. I needed information, and with Danny's systems down, I could turn nowhere else.

"You seek the associate of Jason Magrina." The voice was a flat rumble, but the words were startling in their uncanny accuracy. I tried to keep my face from showing surprise. Alcatraz was not above going for the dramatic effect sometimes, and I hated to give him the satisfaction. I just nodded. "Steve. All I know is the first name."

"Steve Tyrell. He resides under an assumed name at 1141 Catalina, apartment 106."

I blinked. That Alcatraz knew did not surprise me. But that he had divulged the information free of charge did. Alcatraz always had a price – a price usually strange and incomprehensible, such as the death of some individual who obstructed Alcatraz's great plan, whatever it was. I would not have paid such a price, and Alcatraz knew it. But there would be a price, and I knew that. The only question was: what?

"The *satana* is blowing harder." Alcatraz had turned to face the window again. I stared at the stone man's back. Alcatraz never spoke without reason. "It blows death for many. New life for one. And salvation for many more." The stolid face looked back at me impassively. "Go. Now."

As I descended the steps, the wind blew the door shut behind me with a bang. I barely noticed. My mind was a quiet rage. That was the answer, then.

I didn't know how – but I was already paying the price.

21

The blackness of Cutter's enveloped me again at the bottom of the stairs. Though the stairway itself was unlit, the darkness of the bar itself was a palpable force. I squinted through the wind-stirred haze of smoke and stench. On the opposite side from me, a rectangular square of dim orange sunlight marked the door.

And then, suddenly, it went out. Two men blocked the doorway. Men with guns.

Even through the haze, I recognized the silhouettes. Scale and Gordon. The Feds were back.

"L'Hiboux!" They advanced into the bar cautiously, agency-issue 10mm autos swinging nervously. Cutter's was scary enough as it was, and they had learned better than to approach the Owl with weapons holstered. Their eyes blinked, trying to adjust to the darkness. As yet, they hadn't seen me.

There was a slow stirring of anger from the hulking shapes in the dim corners of the room. The regulars were annoyed. No one objected to the guns, but clean suits were practically an invitation to fight in this place. And anyone who wore a *tie* took his life in his hands. The agents wore ties.

Behind the bar, Norbert spat at them. "What you two faggots want?"

Scale swung his pistol at him, producing I.D. with his free hand. "FBI. We trailed a man named L'Hiboux to this place. He came in, and hasn't come out. So we've come in to get him. Where is he?" Scale's voice was ice, though his eyes were bugging a little at the hole in Norbert's head.

Norbert was glowering at Scale's Countess Mara tie. "We don't like ties here, *chingazo*. Lose the fuckin' neckwear."

"Hey! Don't give me *problems*, asswipe!" Scale's teeth were clenched. Gordon was still sweeping the rest of the room with his pistol, trying to spot me in the dark and surly crowd. But I had stepped back into the stairway darkness. Scale leaned closer to Norbert, the auto's muzzle practically against the bartender's greenish nose. He kept his teeth gritted. "I'm looking for the fucking Owl, man. Now, do you cooperate or do I have to *convince* you?"

It was a textbook threat. But this was no textbook situation. Norbert just grinned, his bulbous eyes seeming to give off a faint glow. Pale, scrawny Norbert was Cutter's bartender for one simple reason. All men feared him. And Norbert himself feared no living man. His skeletal grin stretched wider. "Fuck you," he said.

Whap! Scale smacked him on the cheekbone with the pistol, but Norbert paid no attention, snapping a sawed-off 12-gauge from under the bar. *WHOCK!* He sent the agent's pistol flying behind the bar with a blow from the grip as he swung the gun around—

BLAM! Gordon's 10mm cracked like a lightning bolt in the dimness, the magnum hardball slug punching through Norbert's chest. The broken mirror behind him splattered with blood. Norbert slammed back against the wall, fell under the bar. And the Peacemaker in my hand boomed.

KRAKOW! The ·45 slug knocked the auto from Gordon's hand, sailing it into the darkness. Gordon yelled, holding his hand. Scale spun, eyes seeking me across the room. And then he fell under an avalanche of fat, muscle and bone. It was party time at Cutter's.

Sweaty, drunk, diseased and crawling with vermin, the Cutter's regulars had been in and out of prisons all their lives. They had a special hatred for government authority, and for the FBI in particular. Up 'til now, the men in suits had been unreachable, in courts or on the other side of iron cells. But now they were on the floor of Cutter's and it was time to celebrate.

For a moment, I watched indulgently as the great, grunting, hairy mass of brutal humanity pounded, kicked and looted the two yelling agents. Noses were smashed and wallets stolen. But when Dogbutt Sloane pulled a ten-inch sharpened screwdriver from his greasy jacket, I decided to call a halt. Dogbutt was just aiming the gutting tool at Scale's eyes when I blew his leg off at the knee.

"Fuckin' A!" The giant ogre toppled to one side, groping at his shredded jeans. The rest of the brawl stopped dead, everyone looking at me.

I kept the big Colt level, gazing back at them through the wind-swirled muzzle smoke. "That's enough. Let 'em up." There was a stubborn pause, so I cocked the hammer. "Now."

The grumbling swarm pulled back reluctantly, fading back toward the dark tables. Scale and Gordon rolled to their knees, dazed, battered and bloody. Gordon felt at his teeth. Scale could only spit bloody saliva.

I moved to the bar, keeping the gun cocked. A pale hand was clutching at the counter. I grabbed it and pulled Norbert to his feet. "You're dead again."

Norbert nodded dimly, poking a dirty, curious finger into the hole in his chest. It was just to the right of center. No telling what was hit – if it mattered. The blood was a slow ooze. "You get used to it." He tore off a strip from a filthy dishrag and stuffed it into the front and back holes to stop the dripping. Despite the situation, I was curious.

"Does it hurt?"

Norbert poured himself a dirty tumblerful of purple liquid. "Not when you have Jesus." He swilled it down and belched with satisfaction. He was already looking more alert. In the darkness, the Cutter patrons were already regarding him with renewed awe.

I don't know. Maybe the rumors were true.

I turned back to the agents. On the floor, Dogbutt Sloan was examining his shattered leg almost poutingly. "Jesus God, Owl." The fat, denim-clad ogre ripped his jeans open, exposing the splintered wood and twisted hinge. "That leg cost me two hunnerd bucks. Shit."

I tossed him a handful of Jacksons. "Hike, Dogbutt. My call now." I turned to the two agents, keeping my gun cocked. Gordon was on his feet now, unsteadily trying to help Scale up. He watched Dogbutt half-crawl into the shadows and mumbled through bloody teeth: "How'd you know he had a timbershank?"

"I didn't," I said. "Move."

They nodded, dazed and battered, leading the way out into the wind. Even in the alley, the reddish sun was blinding after the darkness of Cutter's. My shades adjusted quickly, but the agents were blinking. At the end of the alley, I stood between them and the sun to enhance the dramatic effect.

"You guys are off your turf," I told them. "Get out of here. And if I were you, I'd forget this place ever existed."

Gordon nodded, helping the still-dazed Scale toward a white Dodge parked not far away. I stepped toward it, intending to wreck the mobile phone, but stopped when I saw the shattered window. No need. The area's unseen residents had been there first.

Scale was bleeding slightly from the ears. Possible concussion, but he'd live. Gordon lowered him into the car painfully. One of Gordon's arms was limp, probably broken. With Scale inside, Gordon leaned painfully against the car, looking at me. Somehow, his attitude seemed different. Saving a man's life will do that sometimes.

"Why the girl, Owl?"

It was a moment to come clean. "She hired me as a bodyguard," I said. "I still don't know what it's about. She's safe at the moment, but the Sandovals seem to want her bad."

It made sense, and Gordon nodded slowly, easing himself into the driver's seat. He shook his head at the hole in the dashboard console. "They're not the only ones." Glancing back at me, he squinted puffy eyes around a broken nose. "How's she paying you?"

I knew what he meant, but my conscience was clear and my face showed it. "Aggravation," I said.

For a moment, he almost grinned. "I can believe it. My daughter's the same age." The car's engine started, and he

143

extended a card out the window. "In case you need it."

It is good for the Owl to have allies, no matter how tenuous. I took the card. "Thanks. Get yourselves to a hospital."

He nodded. "Get back to work."

The car pulled away from the curb and accelerated away as the wind howled.

22

1141 Catalina was an older apartment building in the Los Feliz area, just at the foot of Griffith Park. I spent the better part of an hour circling in on it from a distance, making sure that it wasn't staked out by hostiles from any camp. The fact that I had been spotted and trailed to Cutter's by the Feds still rankled.

The wind moaned uneasily. There was no sign of anything unusual in the neighborhood, but my skin still prickled against the grit. There had been no vans with tinted windows parked casually nearby, no apartments across the street with curtains slightly parted. There were no loiterers of any sort, because of the wind. But I was still uneasy.

The building was a hollow square, glass entrance doors opening to a concrete interior court and swimming pool. California has a million of these, and they are all exactly alike; right down to the windblown dirt in the pool and the fact that the lock on the security doors was broken. I just walked inside.

Apartment 106 was on the ground floor, half-hidden behind a scruffy pampas plant growing from a circle cut in the concrete. I walked around the courtyard twice, checking the other residences. Most were closed up against the wind, curtains drawn and silent, occupants most likely at work. Others were noisy with small children inside, the cheap window-mount air conditioners humming.

My skin still prickled. But I walked up to 106 and tried the door. Locked. And the curtains were drawn. But the air conditioner was going full blast, rattling in time with the windblown pampas plant.

It was 1 p.m., a good two hours before Jason had said to

meet him there. I eased back to the far side of the door and rested my right hand on the Peacemaker's reassuring grip. With my left, I knocked on the door. And waited.

Nothing. I knocked again. All I heard was the air conditioner and the ever-present wind. I felt around in an inside jacket pocket for some bits of steel.

This lock gave me more trouble. I was glad that Sarah wasn't here to make some snide remark. But the force lever turned at last, and I eased the door open.

It was cold inside, the chill air startlingly brisk against skin accustomed to the outside heat. It felt like a refrigerator inside. And for good reason.

Steve was seated in a comfortable chair, smiling at me.

From the looks of things, he had been dead for hours.

The wind whistled hot against the sudden chill in my lower back and I shut the door carefully behind me. The dead man in the chair just kept smiling. I ignored him. Dead men don't bother me. Live ones do. The Peacemaker and I looked for some.

It didn't take long. The apartment was small and sparsely furnished. The bed was a mattress on the floor, and only the bedroom closet was large enough to hide a man. It was open, saving me a precautionary bullet. There was no one else here. I went back to the living room where the dead man held court.

He was young, maybe twenty-five, with sparse blond hair and a thin face. His wallet confirmed that his name was Steve Tyrell, and it wasn't too hard to see what killed him. Scattered over the coffee table in front of him was a soiled Pyrex pipe, a lighter, a square of glass and a small silver bowl full of what looked like rock candy.

Ice. Tyrell had had his date with Crystal, and she had been beautiful. Heart-stoppingly beautiful. I stirred briefly through the glistening crystals in the bowl. Ice was rare in sunny California, and very expensive. Tyrell had been planning himself quite a party.

I moved swiftly around the room, taking in the situation quickly. No T.V., no stereo. A stack of delinquent bills on the kitchen table, most under the name "Tyler Stevens". The man had been an icebird for a while. The only hockable item still in the room was a grubby IBM clone balanced on a rickety writing desk. But the kitchen was the real curiosity. There was a box of Ping-Pong balls on the sink, and a strange contraption made from cardboard boxes and a vacuum cleaner on the floor. The sticky pots on the stove appeared to have been used for mixing chemicals rather than food. I poked at them curiously. Not ice , nor crack; there was no sign of baking soda nor ether. Just a sticky goop, like varnish.

There was another pot on the sink. It was completely empty, except for a slight chemical fragrance. I shook my head – then reacted as the phone rang.

A quick glance told me that Tyrell had at least hung onto his phone machine. The unlit diode indicated that there had been no previous messages. I let the ringing continue. On the fourth ring, the machine picked up. There was a moment of silence, during which I assume Steve's voice assured the caller that he was not at home. I quietly turned up the volume as the machine beeped.

"Hi, Steve," came a melodious whisper. My jaw dropped, then snapped closed again with an angry bang. The voice was Sarah's.

She'd said she didn't know Steve!

The redhead's amplified whisper continued, filling the tiny apartment over the moan of the wind outside. "I'm calling for Jason. Jason, I can't talk long – the Owl left me with his wife, but we're supposed to meet him again at some place called Chaos tonight. I don't think we'll be going by Steve's – the Owl doesn't know where it is, and I didn't think it was a good idea to—oh, shit! Love you!"

The phone went dead with a click and the machine shut off. She must have seen Danny coming. I glowered at the blinking diode for a long moment, angry thoughts seething like red wind in my brain.

Then I began tearing the place apart. I wanted *answers*, dammit, and I wanted them *now*.

The bedroom drawers held a scattered selection of clothes to go with the one good suit in the closet. A diploma from USC in chemistry; some letters from graduate school. Apparently there had been some performance problems. A scattering of family photos, some old coke paraphernalia. No money; not even pocket change.

I checked the suit. There were some movie stubs in one pocket, a plastic squeeze bottle of nasal spray in another. The breast pocket held a plastic I.D. card. I stared at it.

And suddenly, it all made sense.

23

Chaos was an underground L.A. landmark; a big Chinatown nightclub that pretended to be a restaurant and also pretended to be permanently closed. The name was a popular mistake – it was originally owned by a Mr Chao and was supposed to be pronounced *Chow's*. But Mr Chao had neglected the apostrophe from the sign and thus the L.A. punk community had gleefully welcomed the place they pronounced *Kaos*.

They had flocked there in great numbers, slam-dancing in the aisles, putting their own music on the sound system, and intimidating the other patrons. Mr Chao, who had wanted to create a simple, elegant restaurant, had been appalled. He swiftly washed his hands of the whole thing, turning the business over to his nephews. Members of a powerful *tong*, they recognized a good thing when they saw one. They swiftly bricked up the windows, hung "closed" signs all over the exterior, and instituted valet parking. And people flocked there in droves.

Chaos was a place that answered a long-felt L.A. need. You could get anything you wanted there – with enough money. The main floor was for the cheapies looking for a thrill – open tables. They paid a stiff cover charge and got decent food and expensive drinks while they watched strange entertainments; some planned, some spontaneous. The *tong* owners were very aware that L.A. housed a vast number of performance artists, all willing to work for next to nothing if a large audience was guaranteed. Chaos guaranteed the audience, and the drinks were potent. Carried away by the applause, performers had been known to disrobe completely or slash their bodies with knives. The owners were tolerant. Chinatown has its own justice system, and the judges were in the *tong's* pocket.

For the wealthy, though, there were the booths. They were curtained and surrounded the main floor on a raised dias. In the booths you could get *anything*, from opium tea to a skilful blowjob under the table. Sex of the blower was your choice.

Admission to the booths took a stiff tip that varied with the day of the week. It never sank below five hundred bucks, though, not even on a rainy Tuesday. On the other hand, if you had a booth, the food was free.

Danny had gotten a booth. I should have known. I was being punished, as became abundantly clear when the tall Chinese waiter escorted me to the curtained alcove. He was slim and elegant and tightly built under his tux. Sarah, sipping from a tall glass with an umbrella on it, gave him a winning smile. But the waiter merely eased me to my seat and then turned to Danny with a glow in his eyes.

"Should the madam desire *service*," he said, "it would be my honor to provide it. Free of charge."

"Sounds wonderful," Danny said, gesturing under the table. It had been obviously designed for such activity, but I stopped the waiter as he began to draw the booth's curtains. My hand held a C-note. Only raw restraint kept it from being a gun. "Get lost," I said. The waiter took the bill with equanimity and departed. I sat down at the booth, breathing heavily.

Sarah laughed, a delighted titter. "She gave him money to say that."

"I'm aware of that," I said, even though I wasn't. Danny's intense brown eyes gazed at me mockingly over the bourbon Mary. Man, she looked good. Hanging around Sarah for a few days had almost made me forget what a real woman looked like. Lots of smooth curves and interesting bulges. And in Danny's case, a light in the eyes that hinted at dangerous depths. God help me, I was glad I didn't see her often. I had married her for reasons of convenience and legality. She was a Canadian fleeing a murder charge and needing a green card; I was a renegade vigilante needing an associate who couldn't be forced to testify against me.

But as the years passed, I had felt another, very dangerous realization growing.

I was falling in love with her. And I hated every minute of it.

Sarah's laugh interrupted my train of thought. She had new clothes on now; a pair of Guess? jeans and a designer sweatshirt. Pretty, yet practical. She was watching a wildly-painted artist dancing in the aisles, shaking a salami carved like a penis at elderly dowagers. The dowagers were trying to pretend they liked it. "This place is great! You guys come here often?"

"I come no place often," I said. True enough, as far as it went. But at this point in time, I was in no mood to deal with redheaded bimbettes whom I suspected of not having my best interests at heart. I whistled over a tough, powerful-looking Chinese waiter with a surfer's tan. He didn't appear much older than Sarah herself.

"Yeah, dude?"

Born and raised here, obviously. I nodded at Danny. "The lady and I want to be alone for a few minutes." Jerking a thumb at Sarah, I handed the waiter a C-note with my free hand. "Dance with my niece here, okay? Five minutes."

Sarah gave me an angry look, but melted under the admiring gaze from the waiter. "Yeah? Hey, fine by me, man." He extended a tough-looking hand toward Sarah. She rolled her eyes, but began sliding along the seat willingly enough. I rose, allowing her to slide from the seat.

"What's your name, guy?"

"David. David Chen."

"Okay, David. I'm a protective uncle, you know? You keep Sarah safe. Nobody else dances with her, nobody even talks to her, okay? You can handle that?"

The waiter grinned and flipped open his expensive jacket. He had a set of *nunchucks* tucked in his belt. "Hey, we get some wild nights, dude. I can handle anything."

151

"Good." I slapped him on the shoulder and sent them both out toward the dance floor. The performance artists were taking a break, and a DJ was spinning some strange but danceable tunes. Sarah cast a worried, suspicious look back at our booth, but I just waved casually. She and the waiter moved into the small crowd on the dance floor.

"She made a phone call while we were shopping," Danny said in a low voice. "I was paying for her clothes, and she slipped off. I wasn't in time to hear what she said, but she claimed she had just called a friend to say she was all right and not to worry. It seemed reasonable."

I snorted. "She's swift, all right. But I just happened to be on the other end of that call. Not personally – she was talking to an answering machine. But it was in the apartment of a dead icebird named Steve Tyrell."

"Steve?"

"She mentioned him, eh?"

"She was upset, because you two were supposed to meet her boyfriend there about three hours ago. Only you didn't know where it was."

"I knew someone who did," I said. "And obviously, she knew as well. But she was hiding something from me, and she got caught in her own lie."

"What was she hiding?"

I grinned at the sexy, deadly blonde across the table. "You know the rules. What you don't know can't be tortured out of you. Sorry, but it's been keeping us both alive so far." My voice got more serious. "As a matter of fact, as soon as Sarah comes back, I want you to take off. And I mean take *off*. You and Harry. Both vanish for a while, someplace out of state. This situation could get brutal, and I want you out of it."

Danny's eyes flashed darkly, but she turned to look at Sarah and the waiter dancing, halfway across the room. "We had some girl talk. She asked me how I felt about you. I said you were a frustratingly stubborn son of a bitch. She said she felt the same way." The corner of Danny's mouth twitched quirkingly. "It made me feel better. I was glad to know you had *some* moral principles."

I didn't quite know how to answer that, so instead I pulled Sarah's drink over and sniffed at it. Just fruit juice and soda. "She claims to be pregnant."

"It wouldn't show for a while. What's the next step, Al? We've got maybe five more minutes and I've got a hunch that you've been feeling some frustrations of your own." She twitched the curtains meaningfully and her smile became lascivious. "How about a blowjob under the table?"

I swallowed heavily. "I don't think Harry would like that . . ."

"Harry knows the score. He's my boyfriend, you're my husband. Think fast, Al – we don't have much time." She leaned across the table and kissed me, her lips soft, warm and fragrant. Her voice was a warm breeze, a gentle whisper. "I've been practicing. Harry says I'm *really* good now."

I felt the blood pounding in my ears, my eyes losing focus. Danny's soft lips kissed me again. And the Owl's iron resolution crumbled under the sensual onslaught

"Okay," I croaked. Danny's womanly hand reached for the curtains, her lips never leaving mine.

The wall behind the stage blew in with a thunderous crash. And the wind howled in over the screams.

24

Bazooka or LARS rocket, this was a serious hit. Bricks were still sailing through the air, smashing into people and light fixtures as the wind howled through the hole. Danny and I were already moving, guns out, racing as a single team for the dance floor. We plowed through the bleeding people staggering and screaming around the floor tables as a swarm of armed men in black ninja-styled punk garb poured through the hole, carrying a mixture of machine guns and swords.

I slammed against a chunky Hollywood type who was stumbling between two tables, holding a bleeding face and yelling. On the other side of him I could see Sarah lying against one table, her arms clutching her side. Her face was white with shock, contrasting sharply with the blood trickling from a cut on her cheekbone. The waiter, David, was trying to help her to her feet when one of the black-garbed men spotted her. He lunged at her as I swore and shoved my bulky roadblock over a table.

I would have been too late, but David wasn't. *WHICK-WHACK!* His 'chucks flashed from under the jacket and crashed into the underside of the punk ninja's jaw, hard enough to shatter teeth and bone. The ninja wailed, leaping back, and brought up his spacy-looking Steyr AUG machine gun. I blew the left side of his head off, and he fell sideways over a table.

As though that had been a cue, gunfire erupted on all sides. Machine guns hammered sporadically, mowing down various innocent bystanders who happened to be in the way. David belted a sword-swinging ninja punk across the skull, sending him crashing into some empty chairs. And I shoved the Peacemaker away, yanking the dead first ninja's

Steyr away from the body so hard that the black fabric sling snapped.

"Go for the gunners!" I yelled at Danny, spraying a hammering burst of ·223 caliber slugs into a pair of ninjas who were apparently shooting people at random. Danny didn't need my advice. Her blonde hair flying, the ex-pride of the Montreal Personal Protection Agency was saying it with nines. Her Sig was crashing and bucking in her hands, shell casings spinning in the wind as she drilled ninja skulls with the skilled precision of an IPSC action shooter. Her 9mm didn't have the knockdown power of my big Colt, but it held twice as many rounds, and any bullet in the brain is an effective manstopper. She'd taken out eight black-garbed punks in five seconds before they'd realized what was going on. Then they made a point of trying to eliminate her. Danny dove backward over a table as a trio of machine guns tore up the furniture around her, cutting down several screaming bystanders and at least one of their own swordsmen.

The Owl hates sloppy assassins. I emptied the clip from my AUG into the trio, then slammed the hard nylon butt into the black-masked face of a swordsman trying to remove my head. He fell backward over a chair, and I drew the Peacemaker and finished the job. More bullets sprayed by, pounding painfully against my armored back and tearing a chunk out of my right tricep. Fuck it. I spun as I dove for the cover of a fallen table, the Peacemaker booming as I slammed the hammer. Two more ninja gunners sailed backward, their skulls fountaining blood and brains into the wind.

The gunners were down. But the situation was still bad. The Peacemaker was empty, and a second swarm of swordsmen were pouring through the wall into the room. Danny, running up behind me, fired twice more, then swore. Her gun's action held open, empty.

But then, we got help from an unexpected source. From all sides of the room, the tux-clad Chaos waiters leaped forward, flailing *nunchucks* and two-foot razor-sharp *wakazashis*. They charged into the swarm of *katana*-armed punk ninjas in a yelling mass, weapons whirling, smacking and glittering. Blood flew and people yelled.

A swordsman charged me, blade whirling. My martial arts training is limited, but the Owl is a past master at dirty fighting. I caught the sword's swing on the Peacemaker's barrel and used the momentum to help bring my elbow around into the thug's face. Cartilidge crunched and I kneed him in the groin, then brought the empty pistol down on his skull. He dropped as I stepped under another swordsman's swing and helped it continue downward over my uplifted knee. Bone cracked and I swung the Colt back hard, catching a third in the face and knocking him backward over the table.

Danny's black belt showed in her more refined style. Beside me, she spun a swordsman around in an effortless move and wrenched his head sideways. His neck snapped and he dropped like a rag doll. "You really know how to show a girl a good time!" she shouted to me, snapping a stiff-fingered punch into one of the black-clad punks' throat. He sagged, choking on blood.

"Sexual frustration," I snarled back, catching a swordsman's weapon arm and wrenching it around as I lunged behind him. Another sword, intended for me, sliced his head off instead. I shoved the body forward, retaining the sword. The blood spurting from the empty neck caught the other swordsman in the face. He yelled, wiping at blinded eyes, and I jammed the *katana* up through his belly and out between his shoulderblades. His jaw dropped and he fell forward onto his face. I jumped over him, running for Sarah, who was huddled, whitefaced, behind a fallen table. A dead gunner lay nearby. I grabbed for his Steyr first.

"Wo *tong!*" David shouted over the noise. His 'chucks whirled, cracking skulls and arms. "We got a blood feud with these dudes. Fuck 'em, though – they're punks." He decked two ninja thugs in rapid succession.

Punk Chinese *tong* fighters with Austrian machine guns, Japanese swords, and Long Beach accents. That's L.A. I stood, supporting Sarah under one arm and the machine gun under the other. Sarah was biting her lip, tears streaming, trying not to scream. She'd been hurt.

"We have to get out of here!" I yelled at David, cutting through a ninja punk with a three-round burst. He nodded, decking another rival *tong* fighter.

"Side door!" he yelled, pointing. "I'll cover!" Danny ran up to join us, helping to support Sarah as we ran low for the door. Two swordsmen hurtled through the air toward us, but the Steyr took out one and David's 'chuck shattered the arm of the other. They hit the floor in a heap, and I shoved Sarah over to Danny as I kicked the side door open.

Four ninja thugs there, one with a machine gun. About what I expected. We opened fire at the same time, but I had a bulletproof battle jacket and they did not. The ·223 slugs were staggering hammerblows to the chest, but I kept my own muzzle down. The bullpup-style AUG assault rifle flared in a guttural snarl, tearing through the black-garbed punks with screaming copper-jacketed slugs. They tumbled like weeds in the wind, and I threw the empty gun away. Drawing the Waster, I reached to support Sarah again. "Let's go!"

David's chucks were still whirling inside the doorway. "Go ahead!" His grin was white against his tanned skin. "This is my job! Good luck, dudes!" He shattered a ninja arm, and then a skull in rapid succession, and the door closed behind us.

We ran across the parking lot towards Danny's Mercedes. The lot was jammed with people trying to flee and traffic was snarled, fenders banging as people tried to get out. Smoke and noise swirled from the shattered hole in the building wall, blowing away swiftly in the Santa Ana howl. Over it all came the rising tide of sirens, police and emergency vehicles approaching.

One black-clad swordsman had spotted us and was racing across the lot with his sword upraised. I spat at him with the Waster. He kept coming.

"We split up here!" I shouted over the wind and yelling. The swordsman came sprinting up. Danny took a stance, but he simply tumbled at our feet and died. I'd hit him after all. "You take the car!"

"I'm not leaving! Sarah's hurt, and you've been shot—"

So I had. Aside from my arm, one of the ·223 slugs had ducked under the jacket and punched into my hip. Now that she pointed it out, it hurt like blazes. But this was no place to worry about that now. I shut Danny up with an impatient gesture. "The cops'll be stopping everyone trying to drive out. Sarah and I leave on foot. You take the car – they aren't looking for you. Once you get past the cops, pick us up on the corner of 26th and Humbolt. Go!"

Danny looked angry, but got into the car in a seething silence. The wind howled, and drivers near the walled lot's exit blew their horns frantically. Flashing red-and-blue lights were screeching to a halt outside. More gunfire sounded from within the club. Probably police.

The car's engine started. And I ran for the low wall surrounding the rear of the lot, a weeping, whimpering girl tucked under my left arm. I carried her over it and we ran limpingly away into the night, with the sounds of Chaos fading rapidly into the distance behind us.

25

Of course, I had no intention of going anywhere near 26th and Humbolt, and Danny may have known it. Having her part of that mêlée back there had been bad enough. I wanted her safe. She was a capable fighter, but the Owl prefers to work alone. Besides, I had already lost one wife. I wasn't about to lose another.

Still, I knew Danny would be pissed as hell when I didn't show at the rendezvous. I wasn't sure who I was running from more; the police or an angry Danielle Santerre. I wouldn't put it past her to cruise the streets in search of me. So despite the bullet in my hip I kept a forced pace for six blocks before Sarah finally started crying aloud. The tears had been streaming steadily, but the shallow, shuddering gasps of pain could no longer be forced down. Her lips were bleeding from her own teeth. "Owl . . . please . . . God, it hurts . . . !"

We were on Griffin, a few blocks out of Chinatown and away from most of the lights. The area was mostly small houses with Chevys out front; a sign of older Hispanic residents. The wind thrummed steadily through the high-tension wires overhead, occasionally causing a shower of sparks as a wire briefly pulled away from an insulator. I helped her over to the dark stone entryway of an elderly church and eased her to a seat on the steps. She whimpered, arms still wrapped around her side and tears streaming.

The last time I had pulled up the shirt on a sixteen-year-old girl, I had been sixteen myself. Now, a decade and a half later, I found myself on the stone steps of a church, gently lifting the sweatshirt on a beautiful, whimpering, teenage girl while a hot wind howled past the orange moon overhead and sparks of high-voltage electricity flashed and crackled in the night. In the back of my mind, I kept thinking it should be erotic as Hell. But it wasn't. Not with the giant, swollen, purple-and-yellow bruise spreading rapidly across her ribcage. I've had a few broken slats in my time, and I know the signs. When the Wo *tong* had blown open the Chaos wall, she must have stopped a whistling chunk of cold concrete. It was going to hurt for a while.

"I can get you to a hospital," I said, already knowing what the answer would be. Sarah shook her head violently, biting her lip. "No . . . no . . . don't leave me. Have to . . . find Jason."

I nodded, the wind's mocking chuckle echoed in my own dark smile. I pulled my jacket sleeve from the rear pouch. "All right. Let's bandage you up, then."

Individually, the sleeves were too short, but they were equipped with zippers to attach them to the jacket. I used the zippers to fasten the two sleeves together, then wrapped them twice around Sarah's injured ribs. Luckily, the result was an almost perfect length – the two cuffs ends were almost touching. Snugged in tight, I could cross-fasten the cuff snaps, and Sarah's ribs were well bound. I pulled the baggy sweatshirt carefully back down again. The redhead's face was still twisted in pain, but she'd stopped whimpering. "That better?"

She nodded, and I helped her carefully to her feet. She needed rest and recuperation, and this was no place to do it. In these older neighborhoods, the church was open every day for prayers. Prayers we could use, but not the attention. And I had a better idea.

Hollenbeck Park was about twelve blocks to the south of us. Taking a bus or cab would have been nice, but the bullet wounds in my arm and hip were a problem. Though I had done my best to tie them up, they were still oozing in a conspicuous manner. We walked painfully through the night, the hot, irritating wind our only companion.

Sarah's walk was stumbling and forced, her injuries sapping her strength and stamina quickly. She had no energy for talking, and I didn't try to make her. There would be time enough for that later. For myself, I was just trying to keep my right leg moving. ·223 bullets are small, but they're powerful. This one felt like it had punched through my hipbone and lodged somewhere in my ass. Just walking was a constant explosion of fire. But I had to keep moving. The hole wasn't bleeding much, but the leg would stiffen to immobility if I stopped. And at least it made the other hole in my leg seem trivial.

We came in on the north edge of Hollenbeck lurching like Frankenstein's monster and his female captive. The freeway roared nearby and the waves in the stagnant lake were tinged with flame-orange from the moon overhead. There was a boat-rental house on the east side of the lake, nestled under the trees and closed until the weekend. It was a squat, stolid structure scarred with graffiti. The rear extended a short way into the lake and the whole building was stoutly shuttered and locked against vandals.

There was a man asleep against the door, tucked against the side of the entryway most sheltered from the wind, face hidden in the collar of a cheap but clean army surplus coat. I left Sarah in the shadow of the trees and woke him up with a shake on his canvas shoulder. "Scram, buddy."

"Uh?" The head lifted, then turned, blinking blearily. My eyes widened in surprise. It was the same bum I had almost killed on the other side of the lake two nights ago. I almost didn't recognize him. He'd picked up some clean clothes from a surplus outfit, and had managed to get a shower and shave somewhere. Probably a mission. He wasn't even drunk. He rubbed his eyes quickly, then focused on the bill in my hand. Only a fifty this time, but he took it quickly enough. "*Gracias.*" Then he looked up at my face – and his jaw dropped. "*Madre de dios.*"

"*Que pasa*, man?" I said. "You haunting this place?"

"No me – you." His broken-tooth grin was a sporadic flash in the dark as he got to his feet, carefully brushing off his new clothes. "I have job tomorrow. Soon, an *apartamento*."

Well, Hell. I gave him another Grant. "*Buena suerte*," I said. "But *vete*. I desire solitude."

He tucked the bill away, still grinning. "Okay." Turning, he walked away across the park, head up into the wind. I shook my head. At least *somebody's* life seemed to be changing for the better.

Sarah stepped quietly from the shadows, the pain of her injuries temporarily giving way to curiosity. "Was that—?"

"Yeah," I said. The boathouse padlock was irritatingly rusty, but I got it open at last. We stepped through the door into darkness.

The interior of the boathouse was a single large space, the shore end floored with planks and the rest open to the water below. Multicolored fiberglass pedal boats bobbed close together in the water. They were illuminated from below by eerie moonlight filtering through the water under the closed lake doors. A single counter with an old mechanical cash register was the only furniture within the place. The cash register was open and empty.

I helped Sarah lower herself to the floor, lying down on her back with a grunt of pain and an exhausted sigh. Then I spent a difficult few minutes trying to figure out how to refasten the padlock on the outside of the front door. Fortunately, the window shutters were locked on the inside. I opened one, climbed out to padlock the door, then climbed back in and locked the window. By the time I was done, Sarah was sound asleep on the floor, whimpering only slightly as her ribs twinged. As for me, my teeth ached from the clenching I'd given them. Climbing in and out of windows with a bullet in the hip is agony in its purest form.

The wind moaned and the waves it kicked up washed under the lakeside doors, rocking and thumping the little boats in the darkness. A battered Jet-Ski was tethered beside them. Not a rental, obviously – the tow cable attached behind it indicated a more practical purpose. Probably to retrieve pedal boats on the lake that broke or were abandoned by pranksters. It added a faint smell of gasoline to the lake-scented boathouse interior, but there were enough crevices in the walls for the Santa Ana to keep the atmosphere swirling.

I sat down at a large crack between two heavy wall planks, looking out at the shoreline. Orange moonlight played through the crevice. The wind puffed on my face. I slipped an iridescent plastic case from my pocket and turned it in my fingers, letting it glimmer in the night.

The wind outside sighed over the lake.

And Sarah slept.

THURSDAY

26

The wind slowed somewhat in the red light of dawn; the Santa Ana quieter but more ominous. Peering through one of the cracks around the boathouse window, I could tell that the winds were a long way from over. So far, the Santa Ana had been bothersome, irritating and hot. People's nerves were frayed and tempers short.

But it had yet to show what it could *really* do.

Sarah was still asleep on the floorboards, tiny beads of sweat forming, then evaporating on her forehead. The dust that puffed through every crevice settled onto the sweat droplets and stayed. The sight made me wipe my own forehead. It was like running a hand over soggy sandpaper.

I took the iridescent plastic case from my pocket and looked at it once more. Sarah was starting to stir. A sunbeam through one of the cracks was falling on her crimson hair; creeping its way upward toward her face. I found another sunbeam not far away and set the case where it would be illuminated in the most striking way when she awakened.

It was time to cut the shit.

The sunbeam crept over Sarah's eyebrows, glimmered on her lashes, and then sparkled a bright green as her eyes blinked and squinted. She groaned and turned on her side, then yelped as her injured ribs protested. Her eyes blinked again, then were caught by the glistening of the iridescent case. The sun was hitting it perfectly. She gasped and sat up fast, ignoring the ribs in her shock.

"Good morning," I rumbled. I had chosen my stance carefully. There was a large gap in the ceiling boards, and I was standing in front of it. Sarah would see a diagonal bar of red sunlight, with the Owl in silhouette before it.

167

Dramatic and effective. I would need all the psychological edges I could get.

Sarah dove for the case, lifted it, and flipped it open rapidly. The compact's little mirror tumbled out and shattered on the planks. I clicked my tongue sympathetically.

"Seven years bad luck," I said. "You should be more careful."

Sarah's eyes were as hot as the wind. "You bastard. You mutherfucking sonofabitch bastard. Where *is it*?!!" The last words were a guttural shriek. All of a sudden her voice wasn't melodious anymore. She sounded like the girl in *The Exorcist*.

"You mean this?" I pulled a small square of paper from my pocket. "Don't worry. It's safe."

"*Give it!*" Her voice was a sudden shriek above the wind. She hurtled herself across the room, clawing at my hands and face. I backhanded her to the floor with a head-snapping *crack!* Brutal, but I was angry. Ice-cold angry. It showed in my voice, which was unnaturally cold and calm.

"Not a bad trick. You were worried I might turn you over to the police, so while I was gone getting food, you went to the post office and mailed your compact home. Only there wasn't any home. Burned down, and the only survivor was missing. So the Post Office held your mail. Just like you knew they would. Held it until you would show up to get it. Brilliant."

I paused. Sarah was still on the floor, holding her face and glaring at me. Her eyes were laser-green with fury. Behind me, the little boats rocked and bobbed nervously.

"But there's one problem," I said. "The Post Office is not a bank. They don't keep your signature on record, and frankly, they don't like holding mail. So they'll give it to anyone who shows up with a forged note and a passable story. Which is what I did yesterday, just before I went to Chaos."

Sarah's voice was tight and low, a husky growl. "How did you know?"

"While you were with Danny, I was at Steve's." I nodded at her suddenly startled expression. "Yes, I found it. And yes, I was there when you left your message. So was Steve. He's dead, by the way."

She reacted to that – honest shock, as near as I could tell. "You *killed* him!? Oh, God – what about Jason?"

"Your boyfriend wasn't there. And I didn't kill Steve. He did that himself. Ran into an icestorm and just couldn't stop. By the time I showed up, he'd been dead at least a day. But there was enough in the apartment for me to figure out what was happening. Obviously, I'd arrived before Jason showed up to remove the evidence."

I stepped forward into the light, letting the crimson sunlight play over the hard features of my face. My hat kept my eyes in shadow. I held up the paper square.

"So this was what it was all about. This was the reason the Sandovals were chasing you. This was the reason for all the risks, all the expense, all the death." I nodded slowly, looking at the paper in my hand. "It makes sense. Six pounds of coke didn't. But . . . " I savored the words, rustling the innocuous Lottery ticket in my fingers, " . . . thirty-eight million dollars does. That is a lot of reasons."

Sarah's eyes were as hot and dry as the wind outside. "What do you want?"

"Some answers, for one thing. How the Hell did you guys pull it off? And don't tell me luck. That ping-pong ball contraption of Steve's wasn't just a science-fair project. And the numbers are your birth date. I knew they were familiar."

Still on the floor, Sarah shrugged sullenly. "It was Steve, mostly. He'd gotten a job at the Gaming Commission, you know?"

I nodded. The I.D. badge had revealed that. "But he was a speed freak even then, right?"

Sarah shrugged. "I guess. He and Jason were working on something. Anyway, Jason helped him pass the drug tests . . . "

"Who supplied the urine?"

For a moment, she flushed. "I did, yes. You get off on knowing that?"

"Information is always useful. You've told me more in the past three minutes than in the past three days. So Steve got a job at the Lottery."

"Servicing the machine, yeah. Anyway, he figured something out. I don't know what, exactly. Some sort of spray that made the balls rougher or fatter or something. The ones he sprayed wouldn't go through the hole good. The clean ones would."

"The Lottery people wouldn't catch this?"

"I guess they only check the balls that win or something. Anyway, the stuff evaporated fast under the T.V. lights. Jason and Steve figured they were safe enough. But they could only do it once. They rotate the service guys a lot, to keep people from doing stuff like this. Steve's last shot was coming up."

"So they rigged the Lottery. The All-American dream."

"Yeah, well, there was a problem anyway. Steve's thing wasn't perfect. Five of the six balls were pretty guaranteed. But getting all six only happened sometimes. Other balls would get in anyway. Jason and Steve figured they had to cover all the bases."

"Simple enough," I started to say, and then stopped. Sarah was snorting bitterly.

"Yeah, you'd think so, right? Not really. I hate math, but Steve had worked the whole hairy thing out on the computer. They didn't know *which* of the five would show. So they had to buy all the possible combinations, you know? It was a bitch. Over *thirty thousand* numbers."

"So that was what happened to the coke."

"Yeah. Jason and Steve needed money anyway. But they figured it was worth doing. When they won the Lottery, they could pay it back easy."

"How many were involved?"

"Just us four. Me and Allegra, Jason and Steve. Of course, only Jason could collect, because me and Allegra are . . . *were* too young, and Steve works for the Lottery. But we could all buy."

"You four bought thirty thousand tickets?"

170

"That was the bitch. We split up the numbers, went all over the place. Steve and Jason took the most, but Allegra and me got five thousand each, a hundred at a time. She took the west Valley and I took the east. I told people my dad was getting them, he had a system or something. Nobody cared. But it took *forever*. I had to ditch school. They called my parents and I got grounded cold all weekend. My mom even took out my phone." Her eyes looked even angrier for a moment, then she shrugged, running a slim hand tiredly through her red mop of hair. "But, you know, we won, right? And the real pisser is that all six numbers came up after all. My birthday – Jason was sweet."

"Why not Allegra's?"

"Her birthday's like February 5th, you know? Not enough numbers. But Jason was doing it for me anyway. He told me a secret. He was going to pay off the Sandovals and get out of coke dealing. He had a business he wanted to set up, and then, like . . . " Her eyes dropped a little.

" . . . you two could run off to Vegas." The scorn in my voice was obvious. "You're a sap, you know."

"It would have worked!" Her voice was a wail. "But . . . but then—"

"The Sandovals got impatient," I nodded. "That's the problem with getting your financing by ripping off druglords. The repo men they send are tough. Allegra must have spilled the beans before she died."

"Yeah." Sarah's voice was small.

"And the result . . . has been mayhem. Did Allegra know Steve Tyrell?"

"Not really . . . " The voice stayed quiet. "They never met, I think. He was Jason's friend. We used Steve's apartment, sometimes, you know, to meet . . . "

I felt my stomach lurch, but gave no outward sign. *Damn the male ego,* I thought. *I REFUSE to be jealous of the bastard.* But my mind kept remembering Sarah's slim, nude body in the bathroom, and picturing them together . . .

"Ahem." I had to physically shake myself out of it. "What's this business Magrina wants to start?"

"I'm not sure." Her voice was wistful. "Paint production or something. Anyway, he'd be getting out of drugs . . . "

"It's about time," I said dryly.

Her eyes flashed hotly. "Well, at least he doesn't *kill* people for a living!"

"Not directly, no. However, that is not my concern. You are. You've been feeding me a steady line of crap since this began, but it's stopping now. One last question. Are you pregnant?"

She rolled her eyes. "No."

"Fine. So much for my chivalry. Let's put this on a material basis, then. Here's your ticket."

I handed her the slip of paper. She snatched it, checking it quickly and then tucking it away in a pocket. Then she got to her knees, looking at me suspiciously. "What do you want?"

"Payment. I charge two years' income. It's a fair sliding scale that cripples almost anyone. People who hire me had better *really* want my services. And you hired me. So I'll get you to your boyfriend – but then I get paid. After taxes, that ticket will pay one point five million dollars a year over the next twenty years. So I get three million."

"Oh, for God's sake . . . !"

"Don't argue. I have a reputation and a price. I was hired, now I get paid. Magrina almost certainly intends to sell the ticket or borrow money against it anyway. He'll easily get over twenty million. I will give him a month to come up with my three. Let him know that. And tell him not to cross me." My smile was a deadly glint. "Or he'd better give up sleep."

"You bastard!" She tried to stand, but winced painfully. Holding her ribs, she sat down again.

"Oh, shut up." I turned away dismissively. There was a worn flannel shirt hanging from a nail beside the cash register. I pulled off my battle jacket and the twin shoulder holsters beneath. "You're still alive, which is more than I can say for your friend, your family, and a lot of other people. You and your boyfriend have a ticket worth thirty-five

172

million bucks, even after my payment. And *I'm* the one
with the bullet holes."

I winced, unbuttoning the bloodstained shirt I was wearing. The clotted blood had stuck the cloth to the arm wounds,
and I gritted my teeth as I ripped the shirt loose. Blood
started oozing again, but I bandaged the torn flesh with new
strips cut from the shirt. It hurt like sin, but I had no choice.
I couldn't go out looking like a hunting accident. I carefully
shrugged into the flannel shirt, letting the ends hang down
as I replaced the weapons and jacket. It looked sloppy, but
it concealed some of the blood on my hip.

The pain in Sarah's ribs had caused her to lay down again.
She had fished the ticket out and was examining it carefully,
making sure I hadn't pulled some sort of switch. Money like
that makes people paranoid, especially when it is all wrapped
up in a single piece of paper. Apparently satisfied, she rolled
her head over to look at me. "You going somewhere?"

"Yeah." I moved painfully over to the window and undid
the lock. "You want your boyfriend and I want my money
– now that I know about it. I'll arrange a meeting. You'll be
safe if you stay here." I opened the window shutter, peering
out. The hot morning wind stirred the trees overhead.
No one was in sight but a distant jogger. I clambered
outside, gritting my aching teeth again on the agony. "I'll
be back later."

Sarah had managed to get to her feet, staggering and
wincing. "Could you, like, bring some food?"

I nodded coldly. "No problem." A thought struck me. "By
the way. If I do reach Magrina, he doesn't know my voice
well. You two have a code word or something? Something to
convince him he'd really be meeting you, and not a Sandoval
reception committee."

Sarah's face twisted, thinking. Then she nodded, smiling
a little shyly. "He, um, gave me a pink rose . . . after our
first time. It was so romantic . . . "

"Right." My voice was sharper than I intended. I fought
it under back control. "Yeah. Okay, I'm leaving now. Lock
the window so no one gets in." I shut the shutter, then

peered through the crack. Still half-dazed with pain, she fumbled the latch closed and pushed the padlock shut with an audible click.

I nodded, satisfied, and turned away. Locking the window meant more than keeping strangers out.

It kept her from running away before I got back.

Some people will do anything to save a lousy three million bucks.

The first thing I did was lurch through the wind to a nearby tropical fish store. Los Angeles is full of them – which is a convenience for outlaws like myself, occasionally suffering from a case of bullet holes. Hospitals and doctors are a last resort, since they report such things to the police. But if the wounds are not in a vital organ nor bleeding excessively, you can get by without treatment for a long time – if you can beat infection. And that's tough. Deep wounds get infected easily, and antibiotics like penicillin are a prescription drug.

For humans, that is.

But fish get infected too, and nobody takes their guppy to the vet. So, conveniently enough, you can buy capsules of sulfa or penicillin right off the rack at any good fish store. They're not made in FDA-approved conditions. But they work. One capsule for every five gallons. A two-hundred-pound man is the approximate equivalent of a twenty-gallon tank. I bought a good supply from the Korean proprietor and swallowed four tabs on the way out. A gaudy, flame-red Siamese fighting fish spread his fins aggressively at me from his tank.

Even under water, he was feeling the wind.

I walked limpingly to a phone booth down the block, dropped in a quarter and dialed from memory. My lips tightened in silent prayer. I'd only seen the number once, and briefly.

The phone clicked, buzzed once, and Steve's answering machine picked up. I'd remembered the number printed on his unpaid AT&T bill correctly.

"Hi, this is Steve. I'm not available right now, but . . . " The usual spiel. I waited until the beep, then spoke in my most cool and dangerous voice.

"Hello, Magrina. This is the Owl. I know you're hiding out there. Your dead buddy didn't crank that air conditioner himself. I'd advise you to pick up."

The phone clicked even as I finished. I heard Jason's voice speak, tinged with wary caution. "What do you want?"

"Sarah wants to meet with you. She can't call herself – she got hurt last night. Not bad, but she has to lay low for a while. I'm keeping her safe."

"Uh . . . how do I know this?"

"She said to tell you about a pink rose."

"Huh? Oh, yeah. Okay."

Romantic. "You willing to meet her tomorrow?"

"Uh . . . "

"She said to tell you that everything's set."

"Yeah?" The voice suddenly sounded a lot more eager, which was not surprising. "Yeah, great. Where? Is she okay?"

Belated concern. Girls can sure pick 'em sometimes. But it was none of my business. I stuck to what was. "She'll meet you at Hollenbeck Park. Center of the lake bridge at noon tomorrow. Got that?"

"I'll be there."

"Come alone," I growled, and hung up the phone. The wind blew hot breath across my face as I fished in my pockets for more coins. On top of the booth, a dusty spider web stretched from booth to wall, bellying like a sail in the wind.

Out of quarters. I dug a handful of change from the depths of my pocket and spread it in the crimson dust atop the booth. Thirteen dimes and seventeen nickles. They winked redly in the sunlight as I stared at them sourly. Under the circumstances, thirty pieces of silver was appropriate as Hell.

The spiderweb atop the booth tore, flapping in the wind. I dropped in a couple of dimes and dialed.

FRIDAY

27

The sun rose like a hot copper ball in the eastern sky, the wind howling before it like demons heralding the coming of Satan. The trees bent and quivered before the gale, the roasting heat already stripping away what little water was left in their leaves. It was 6 a.m., and the day promised to be pure Hell.

Sarah was still asleep, stretched out on the floor amongst the Burger King trash. I'd given her some of the antibiotics, and since she wasn't pregnant, I'd followed her lunch with aspirin and Sominex. Kept the heat and pain from driving her nuts. She'd been asleep for sixteen hours, which was just as well. She probably needed it. Besides, it kept her out of my hair. I'd had work to do.

As I expected, people had started drifting around the park at a fairly early hour. A good supply of gardeners, dog walkers, and fruit-ice vendors had shown up practically at daybreak. I watched with some amusement from crevices between the boathouse walls. Hollenbeck would have looked as good as the Huntington if it really had that many gardeners. But after a short time somebody got organized and things thinned out. Only a couple of desultory coverall-clad Hispanics moved around the dry grass, raking futilely at the windblown leaves and trash.

They were waiting for us to show up. What they didn't know was: we were already here.

I sighed, sipping cold coffee from a styrofoam cup. Calling the feds had been a difficult decision, especially for the Owl. A night of chewing it over hadn't made it taste any better. If she'd been a little bit older, maybe I'd have just taken my money and walked away from the whole thing. But, damn it . . .

I turned, easing myself with painful stiffness to a seat on the floor. The hot wind whistled through the crevices, stirring Sarah's scarlet locks on the dusty planks. Her small face was peaceful in its slumber, glowing faintly in the dim light within the boathouse. And the Owl watched over her, broodingly.

I'd said I would *protect* her, damn it, and that was what I was going to do. Sixteen was too young for an orphan girl to decide to run off with a drug dealer boyfriend and a rigged lottery ticket. Magrina's actions so far had hardly indicated he was a stable type. He'd tire of her in less than a year, and then what? Prostitution maybe, death probably. She would know too much for him to be comfortable with her alive.

So I'd called. I'd told them nothing; only that Sarah would be meeting her drug dealer boyfriend. The FBI would arrest them both, and the whole story would come out. The creep Magrina would go to prison on a variety of charges, which was just fine with me. Sarah, however, was a minor. She'd killed, but shooting an assassin in a defense situation with the assassin's own gun was hardly prosecutable. If she turned state's evidence, she'd get off with probation. The FBI would set her up under the Witness Protection program. She'd end up somewhere far away, with a new name and a new life.

Another chance. A lot more than she had now.

I frowned sourly into the dust floating in my coffee cup. Too bad the decision would cost me three million bucks. And I wasn't entirely sure how I was going to get out of this myself. But I'd taken certain precautions in the night. Among other things, a handsaw, hand drill and eyebolts purchased at a local hardware store had been put to several hours hard use. I rubbed my blistered palms together painfully. I'd just have to hope for the best.

The clustered boats bobbed and thumped in the dimness. And the wind chuckled mockingly.

It was a little after nine o'clock when Sarah stirred, blinking her eyes in a lost manner at the ceiling planks overhead, then suddenly remembering. She tried to sit up, but her face twisted in agony before she'd even raised her shoulders. She clutched at her side. "Owwwww."

"Here." I extended a couple more Tylenol and a half-empty bottle of flat Perrier. She took them gratefully and managed to get the pills down without spilling more than a third of the water into her nose. Her coughs and snorts were interspersed with wails as the ribs put up a fight.

"Easy. Easy." I moved over fast, holding her head as she sneezed out the rest of the water and then whimpered as the ribs protested the chest activity once more. "Sorry. I should have helped you sit up first."

"It's okay." The elfin head turned, green eyes regarding me seriously. "You're my bodyguard. I don't expect you to be my nurse, too. You've already done so much for me. I want you to know – I really appreciate it."

Her voice was soft and honestly grateful. I felt like a total pile of shit. "That's sure a different tone than yesterday," I growled suspiciously.

"You were right – I needed sleep," she admitted. "I still don't know how you do without it. I kept trying to keep up with you, and I was, like, half-dead. I'm sorry. What time is it?"

"Nine-thirty." I said. "You and your boyfriend should be back together in two and a half hours." *And taken in by the Feds shortly after that*, I muttered to myself silently.

Sarah sighed dreamily and reached over to rest a slim hand on one of my grubby sneakers. "God, I can't wait. It's like a movie or something. We'll be young and in love – and rich." Her green eyes blinked at me sadly. "I'm sorry you never got to really know Jason. Maybe you can, later. You'll like him."

"Uh, hunh."

Her lips twitched in a smile. "Oh, stop being grouchy. You'll get your money. I promise."

I was feeling worse than ever. "What about the Sandovals?"

Sarah's trim eyebrows crinkled a little, worriedly. "Well, Jason can pay them back for the coke. Plus interest. Then we'll vanish for a while. But they'll still be after you, I guess." Her eyes clouded. "I'm really sorry."

I didn't look at her. "What the hell," I said. "Three million bucks will be pretty fair compensation."

My words sounded hollow, but she didn't seem to notice. She just nodded slightly, watching the red sunbeams flicker as the wind tossed the trees outside. After a long silence, she spoke again. "Owl?"

"Don't call me that," I muttered automatically. Sarah's smile was a soft glimmer of white in the dimness. She pulled at my shoelace diffidently.

"Owl . . . ? Would it . . . Would it really have been so bad . . . you know, if we had . . . if we had made it?"

"Terrible," I said, and meant it. I felt bad enough as it was.

There was a moment of silence, and then Sarah sighed again, a strange melodious harmony with the wind outside. "Well, anyway, I'm sorry about the Sandovals."

"Don't sweat it," I said, the sick feeling worse than ever.

I'd called them, too.

28

The wind was a blistering furnace and the angry red sun glared straight down from overhead. The gardeners – whoever they were – were leaning limply on their rakes under the shade of an old cypress, letting the roasting wind strip the sweat from their brows. They actually looked more natural that way. It was what real gardeners would have been doing.

I had spent the last couple of hours in a nervous, limping pace, keeping a lookout from various cracks. People drifted through the park. A couple of them had investigated the boathouse, but the padlock on the outside of the door had kept anyone from feeling a pressing need to check inside. And the wind howled over everything.

Three minutes to twelve. A long gray limo caught my eye, easing to a stop in the parking area across the lake, just this side of the freeway embankment. Enrique Sandoval himself, as I had expected. For this kind of money and this kind of vengeance, the boss shows up personally.

And then I saw something else. A tall young man, with a twitchy, cautious gait, crossing the park at a nervous lope. He looked pale, and the wind itself seemed to make him jump.

"Up you get," I said to Sarah. "Your boyfriend's here."

Magrina's twitchy nervousness was obvious as he got closer. He practically jumped out of his shoes as a jogger passed close by him – probably the only legitimate visitor in the park. He ran a hand through his hair nervously, twice, then stepped warily onto the bridge as though it would collapse underneath him.

I was holding Sarah upright in my arms. Her cheek nestled gently against my chest. "Okay," I said. "It's time."

She nodded, then reached up with her left hand and pulled my head down gently. She kissed me on the cheek.

"Thanks for everything, Owl," she whispered.

I pushed on the door. The padlock latch fell away from the outside. I had removed the nuts from within last night. "No problem," I said.

She stepped out alone into the wind.

From the dimness of the boathouse I saw her move painfully toward her side of the bridge. Jason was already halfway across the other side, looking around with increasing suspicion. They saw each other at the same time.

"Jason!" I could hear her voice, a melodious song over the wind. Despite her injuries, she bounded toward the bridge like a young gazelle, prancing along its concrete length. Magrina, trying to be cool, met her at the center with his arms outstretched. "Sarah, Jesus, thank God . . . "

They kissed. I felt my guts wrench with guilt. But I had other worries. From the trees surrounding the boathouse, I could see several men that were formerly gardeners and fruit-ice sellers moving toward the building cautiously.

I risked a last glance toward the bridge. Sarah was giving Magrina the ticket. Everything was going as I planned. In a few moments they would leave the bridge, and the Sandovals would attempt to abduct them. Then the FBI would step in, arresting everyone. I anticipated a certain amount of confusion, during which I planned my escape. In Enrique's limo, with any luck. I had made a promise regarding him – a promise I intended to keep.

It would have been rough, though I still think I could have pulled it off. But then suddenly something went horribly wrong.

On the bridge, Margrina finished checking the ticket and put it in his pocket. Sarah, face beaming and scarlet hair flying in the crimson wind, stepped toward him for another kiss.

And Magrina, pulling a ·44 Magnum from inside his belt, blasted four thundering slugs into her heart.

I know I yelled, but I didn't hear it. All I heard was the eerie wind as Sarah, face white and eyes bulging, slammed back against the bridge rail. Blood bubbled in a stark scarlet froth from her mouth. Her face showed no pain, only confusion and betrayal. She fell forward onto her face.

And all hell broke loose.

The first thing I heard was the *crunch* of the Peacemaker's barrel as I rammed it through the boathouse wall, trying to aim through a tiny crevice. *BOOM!* I'm good, but not that good. The crevice kept the angle wrong, and the slug merely fountained a gush of water into the air. The wind caught it and whipped it over Magrina's face. Galvanized into action, he started to run.

Phut!Phutphutphut!Phut! The familiar spitting sound of Sandoval ·22s hammering at his heels was quickly drowned out by a new sound. *BAMMABAMMABAMMABAM!* From other sides of the park, FBI sub-Uzis and 10mm autos began mowing down startled Sandoval hitmen. Others began firing back.

Three of the gardeners came running for the boathouse, guns extended. Time to get out of here.

The Jet-Ski roared into life with the kick of a throttle, and I blasted out the lakeside doors at a slit-churning roar just as the gunmen ran inside the boathouse. The Jet-Ski's towing cable trailed behind me, connected to a series of pins inserted in holes in the rafters. *Whickwhickwhickwhickwhick!* The pins were yanked free in rapid succession, leaving the beams – which I had sawed through, one by one, the night before – with no support. The ramshackle roof creaked . . . then fell in with a resounding crash. I couldn't hear the yells over the Jet-Ski's motor, but I knew they were there.

Magrina was nowhere in sight, but the gray limo was already moving, swinging a wide arc in the parking lot.

Bullets, fired from all sides, tore up the lake around me, but I ignored them. I dragged back a steel hammer with a blistered thumb.

BOOOM! The Peacemaker bucked, slamming a half-inch chunk of lead through the limo's hood. I got lucky. It smashed through the radiator and split open the fuel injector. With a hiss and a *Whoom!* the engine went up in flames.

Sandoval leaped out, his pudgy face florid and a massive .44 Desert Eagle in his hand. Apparently, he left the shrimp calibers to his underlings. An FBI agent ran toward him and Sandoval's gun thundered. The muzzle flash was the size of a soccer ball. The agent flipped in the air and was dead before he hit the ground. Sandoval began running for the distant freeway embankment. From the saddle of the racing Jet-Ski, I was already taking aim with the Peacemaker when a 10mm slug blew through the aluminum engine block. The Jet-Ski cartwheeled, and I hit water with my face. It knocked the breath out of me, which was just as well, since I was under water and couldn't breathe anyway. Bullets splatted into the shallow water above my head, tearing gossamer traces in the grimy lake. I decided to stay under a while.

The Peacemaker was still in my hand. I clumsily holstered it again, staying as low in the silt as I could. The lake was only four feet deep, and bullets were still streaking through the water around me. Sandoval would be out of range by this time anyway. I cursed a bubbling stream.

Then my swirling fingers touched carpet. I scrabbled at it, my lungs bursting and my eyes blind in the dark water. From seemingly far away, I saw the silver gleam of stainless steel.

God damn.

With desperate urgency, I wrenched the rifle free of the cloying carpet and ripped the bolt back. Then I got my legs under me and shot to the surface.

I came out of the water like a sounding whale, water pouring down the barrel of the gleaming steel rifle in my hand and out the open bolt. Three days under water hardly bothers stainless steel and fiberglass at all. I racked the bolt home, a four-inch-long ·308 round slamming from the magazine into the chamber.

A ·22 bullet pounded into the back of my sodden battle jacket. But the dripping rifle was at my shoulder, and the crosshairs of the waterproof Leopould had settled on the distant target. Enrique Sandoval had just reached the edge of the distant freeway when the rifle slammed back against my shoulder, the muzzle kicking skyward.

I was a little off. The slug blew a chunk out of Enrique's knee. He screamed, a distant keening, and fell.

Onto the freeway. The gravel truck's driver stood on the air brakes, but there was no way to stop in time. Two sets of double wheels ground the fat, criminal swine Enrique Sandoval to a bloody pulp and threw the remains to the wind.

And the Santa Ana howled.

More ·22s splashed water around me. I whirled in the lake, seeing a pair of Sandoval thugs firing at me from shore. I knocked one into a blood-spraying cartwheel with the ·308. And FBI agent Gordon, one arm in a sling, took out the other with his 10mm.

"Owl!" He was gesturing as he shouted, waving his pistol behind me. "He's getting away! My men are down!"

I turned. The freeway above the lake was an ungodly, horn-blowing snarl. And scrambling up the embankment toward it was Jason Magrina. Somehow, he'd made it through the firefight.

I snarled. The rifle leaped to my shoulder, but the firing pin just thunked. The last shell had taken water. Damn! I threw the rifle away and churned toward the shore as Magrina vaulted the freeway railing and vanished from sight.

Climbing that hill was agony with the bullet holes in my calf and hip, but I did it at a dead run, twice as fast as either Magrina or Sandoval. The Owl's legs are like iron wings.

Hurdling the four-foot fence at the top, I landed on the freeway with a soggy splat and a snarl. The sopping wet

Peacemaker was in my hand, searching for a target.

Too late. The aghast driver of the gravel truck had stopped dead on the freeway to confirm his own horrified senses. The rest of the traffic had snarled up behind him. Now the truck driver, having gotten out to see what was left of Enrique Sandoval, was vomiting over the railing into the lake. And Jason Magrina was stealing his truck.

The Peacemaker crashed, but it was no use. The gravel truck was thick steel, and the slug merely dented the side before careening away into the wind. The truck roared off with a grinding of gears, and I sprinted across the asphalt to the rest of the traffic jam.

A young, wealthy-looking kid was perched interestedly on a Kawasaki Ninja in the third lane, cheerfully rubbernecking the bloody remains of the ex-druglord. He reacted in a gaping double no take as a filthy, blood-covered, mud-soaked Owl stepped up to him, with a snarl on his face and a gun in his hand.

"Loan me your bike," I advised him.

"Good idea," he agreed, sliding nimbly from the vehicle. I swung into the seat before the low-slung racer even had time to teeter. A touch of a button and the engine fired.

I left a smoking trail of rubber as I peeled into the distance. The wind whipped the acrid smoke after me.

It smelled like vengeance.

The Kawasaki was a sex machine, a racing bike that was built for speed alone. I bent low over the cowling and kept the throttle wrenched, my lips peeling back from acceleration and rage. I was doing a hundred and thirty in less than twenty seconds. The speedometer stopped there, but the bike kept going. The engine's scream was a scarlet song of blood and joy, a perfect accompaniment to the rage of red behind my eyes.

The truck was just ahead.

Magrina had seen me coming. He leaned from the window, a ball of fire suddenly appearing in his fist. The ·44 slug smashed a divot in the asphalt ahead of the bike, and flying gravel ripped a gash in my cheekbone. I slowed slightly, steering the bike over behind the truck. Magrina couldn't shoot me here – the truck's bed was in the way. I wrenched the throttle down hard again.

He couldn't shoot, but he had other weapons. The truck's bed suddenly lurched upward. A giant pile of gravel hit the road right in front of me. There was no way to even slow down.

The bike's nose hit the gravel and stopped dead. At over one hundred miles an hour, I went tumbling through the air.

29

The wind was stronger here. Hotter, too. The flat plain of
the Mojave, dotted with dried sage and sargasso cacti,
offered little resistance to the mysterious winds. They blew
unimpeded, hot and dry as death. Behind the lumbering
gravel truck, the sun set like a flare from Hell against the
low mountains on the otherwise featureless horizon.

A flat building off an unmarked road, the asphalt cracked
against the scorching sands, or in many places, missing
altogether. The building is marked in fading, pockmarked
letters against the sand-colored concrete walls: INDUS-
TRIAL PIGMENTS, INC.

It is a good sign. Dull, uninviting, vaguely ominous.
Strange chemicals may be at work here. A good thing to
be far out in the desert. A battered chain-link fence is there,
no doubt for the protection of innocent stragglers.

The gravel truck pulls up to the gate and toots a blast
on its air horn. A swarthy man steps from a shady shack
and squints through the red wind at the truck. He carries
a machine gun. Curious – but the desert has rattlesnakes.
Perhaps it is merely a safety measure.

At a word from the driver, the swarthy man opens
the gate and steps toward the back of the truck. A battered bed, half-full of gravel, nothing more. The swarthy
man shrugs. The driver waves, and rumbles through the
gate.

At the building itself, other men rattle open the truck bay
doors, the dusty galvanized steel taking on the color of dried
blood in the sunset light. Some of the men are dark-skinned
Hispanics, others are Oriental. The wind is still blowing,
and the men curse at the dust. Oddly enough, they too

190

*have machine guns. Perhaps this area is prone to swarms
of rattlesnakes.*

*The men close the bay doors again and place their
machine guns in careful racks. Then they return to their
work. Steel cauldrons cook over electric heaters, piping
fluids through coiled tubes of copper. The making of pigments is a mysterious business. Especially since the small
cauldron at the end is a rapidly-forming vat of something
with no color at all. The smell of ether is strong here, vented
off by powerful fans to be collected and used again.*

*And in the vat below the fans, strange crystals form. They
look sweet, innocuous, like a child's rock candy. And they
are clear as water.*

As clear as – ice.

*The truck's driver looks into the vat, selects a crystal with
fingers trembling from fatigue. He presses it into a glass
pipe and moves toward an interior office, fumbling in his
pocket for a lighter.*

*In the back of the truck, there is a rattle. The pile of gravel
has moved slightly.*

30

I eased myself from the back of the truck as silently as
possible, the Peacemaker in my fist. I had to stifle a
few groans. Travelling sixty bumpy miles in a truck full
of sun-baked pea gravel is hardly first-class transport. I
felt like every inch of my body had been worked over with
red-hot ball-peen hammers.

There was no one in the immediate vicinity. Down toward
the other end of the building I could see a couple of Mexican
men working at a series of small vats. A few Orientals were
supervising. It was hard to tell from this distance, but I could
bet they were Chinese. The air within the building was
incredibly hot – probably close to 150 – and heavy with the
pungent smell of ether, despite the rattling exhaust fans.

Outside, in the darkness, I could hear the wind howl.

In a rack beside the truck bay doors were four space-age
Steyr machine guns. They had an inviting look. Keeping to
the shadows, I holstered the Colt and moved over to the
rack, selecting a pair of nice ones. I also took the loaded
magazines from the other two guns. The magazines were
semitransparent plastic; curved, heavy and slick. They made
a comforting weight when tucked into my belt. I stalked from
the shadows with a machine gun under each arm and five
pounds of ammo in my belt, looking vicious and cool. I just
hoped my pants wouldn't fall down.

The first one to spot me was one of the Mexican workers
near the closest vat. He did a startled doubletake, then
moved with lightning swiftness. I almost blew him away
before I realized he was raising his hands frantically in
surrender. Probably an illegal just working for the money.
I gave him a silent snarl and gestured with the gun muzzle.

He nodded frantically and dashed for an outside door, whistling to his buddy. The other Mexican turned and basically reacted the same way as the first.

But the whistle had attracted the attention of the other men in the room. Closer now, I could see they were Chinese thugs in punk garb. Wo *tong*, for sure. And they didn't look pleased to see me. Two of them dove behind the vats, scrabbling for racked weapons visible on the other side of the room. The third produced a ·357 Smith from his hip pocket and fired it at me.

That was more like it. I cut loose with both barrels and blew him in half. Then I sent a line of slugs across the vats, cutting through an ether pipeline and sending a spray of clear fluid toward the men behind. In the heat of the building, the stuff evaporated before it even hit the ground.

But that just made it more dangerous. They had their own machine guns now and one of them raced forward, screaming curses in Chinese. The muzzle of his Steyr was flaming furiously, hammering bullets in my direction. He ran through the place where the ether was vanishing and suddenly disappeared behind a flash of fire and a thunderous *BANG!* It must have blown his lungs out – the charred body toppled face forward to the floor and burned.

Flames were roaring up now from the ether line, and the temperature in the room was increasing rapidly. Bullets blasted from behind a stack of empty drums on the other side of the vats. The Chinese gunner was concealed behind them, trying to nail me with a series of three-round bursts.

I hit the floor and rolled, coming up on the other side of the vats as another burst of slugs crackled past my ears. He had to worry about his ammo supply. I didn't. I squeezed the triggers of both Steyrs and held them down. *BAMMABAMMA-BAMMABAMMABAMMABAMMABAM*—! Copper slugs tore a gaping hole in one steel drum, then through the one behind it. The *tong* gunner was behind the third. A sudden scream told me I'd gotten through.

Both Steyrs were empty. I threw one aside and reloaded the other. Just in time, too. The *tong* thug had been hit, but

he wasn't dead. He came scrambling out from behind the
drums with his AUG hammering, screaming like a maniac
and bleeding profusely. A suicide charge. My Steyr fulfilled
the last requirement and his body tumbled to a heap among
the metal vats.

The ether was still burning and the wind moaned and
gusted outside. I got cautiously to my feet and went looking
for Jason Magrina.

He wasn't hard to find. The building was mostly empty
space, the crystal meth equipment a small-scale operation
at the moment. Other than the bathroom, there was only one
other room in the whole building. This was a small office set
in one end, its door closed. As I stalked toward it, I heard
a crashing of glass inside.

I didn't waste time trying to kick open the locked and
probably barricaded door. I just turned and raced through
the flames for the building's outer door.

Outside, a full, blood-red moon shone faintly through the
howling hurricane of hot sand and darkness. Dimly seen
through the crimson grit was a tall form, running frantically
for the cyclone fence surrounding. He hit it with arms and
legs flailing, began to scramble up.

I took my time aiming the Steyr's built-in scope, squinting
through the windblown sand. The ·223 kicked against my shoulder, a three-round burst cutting through the Santa Ana night.

And Jason Magrina tumbled to the ground, shot in both
legs.

He was shrieking as I limped slowly toward him,
dragging a week's worth of my own injuries like a heavy
weight. He was clutching at his legs with one hand while he
fumbled out the heavy ·44 Magnum with the other. I kicked
it contemptuously from his hand.

"Stick to shooting girls," I told him. "It's what you're
good at."

He was shrieking again, his eyes as hot and red and wild
as the moon above. His screeches were barely coherent, and
seemed driven more by mindless fury rather than pain. "You
bastard! You *bastard*! You fucking *bastard*! You fucking

shot me from *behind*, you chickenshit prick! I'm calling my lawyer! You've got no right—"

He broke off then, because I had kicked his teeth in. He thrashed on the ground for a moment, holding a face that was no longer handsome.

"Spare me," I growled, the tired anger in my voice carrying even over the wind. "You know who I am. You're a dead man, Magrina."

He rolled, spitting a handful of bloody teeth into the wind-blown dirt. I kept the gun trained, looking down at him.

"I should have known earlier," I said. "I kept wondering at those things that didn't fit. The two thugs at Sarah's house, for instance. They weren't Sandoval regulars. Wrong guns, for one thing. And one of them left a message on your phone machine. *You* hired them. You had her parents killed."

He was half-sitting in the dirt now, fumbling out a little Pyrex pipe from his pocket. "Bitch was trying to rip me off." His voice was as sloppy as his mouth.

"That's what you must have thought, right. The Lottery is held Saturday night. She was holding the winning ticket, but she doesn't call that night, nor the next day. You probably try to call her, and her parents hang up on you. By Monday, you figure she and her parents have conspired to keep the money, and you decide to do something about it. You still have plenty of cash from the six pounds you ripped off Sandoval, so you pay a couple of hitmen to go get the ticket – by whatever means necessary.

"But there was a couple of things you didn't know. The first was that Sarah wasn't ripping you off. She'd been grounded for missing school on those days she was buying tickets for you. The second thing you didn't realize is that Enrique Sandoval had gotten upset enough about the stash you ripped off to take hard action. His goons grabbed Allegra and did unpleasant things. Allegra didn't know much, but she did know that Sarah had a ticket worth thirty-eight million bucks that you would collect. And by the time Allegra died, Enrique knew it too. That was why his goons were trying to intercept Sarah at school before she even got home."

Magrina had fidgeted a lumpy crystal into his pipe and was trying with difficulty to get his lighter to stay lit beneath. The wind kept blowing it out. "S-shit. I knew they'd gotten Allegra, yeah. But Sarah . . . shit." He got the pipe going and inhaled deeply. "I didn't know she was g-grounded. God, I-I'm sorry. I thought she was set-setting me up. I . . . I shouldn't have killed her. I was crazy." He ran his hands nervously through his sleek hair. "God. I'm really sorry."

I eyed him with contempt. "Crap, Magrina. You read the papers, you talked to her. You knew she was trying to get you the ticket. But with Steve dead, she was the last person who knew the details of your scam. You meant to kill her. You'd always meant to."

Magrina's eyes lashed at me, his teeth grinding from the speed. He'd probably been awake for days, wired up, watching for Sandovals over his shoulder. And maybe somebody else . . . "You can't prove that. Go ahead and take me in. It won't stand up in court."

I just laughed, the wind gusting behind me. "So what!? It's true and we both know it. And I'm the Owl, Magrina, not a cop. The court's right here. Tonight."

"Shit! I have rights—"

"So did Sarah. So did her parents."

"*Christ!* Cut me some fucking *slack*, man!" His voice was a sudden, nervous shriek in the wind. He gripped wildly at the cyclone fencing, trying to pull himself upright. "I just needed the *money*! Fucking Sandoval was a prick, okay? He was leaning on me. I had ambition, you know? I could destroy him someday. He knew that. He *knew* that! He wouldn't let me get *on*, man. Kept me down. So Steve and me set up this place. I had connections, he knew the chemistry." His voice grew more fervent, intense. If not for the dryness of his mouth in the desert, he'd have been foaming. He was half-standing now, legs flopping beneath him, clawing himself upward on the fence. His almost pupil-less eyes stared at me with glassy conviction.

"Ice is *hot*, man! Kicks ass on crack, and you don't have to deal with any greaseball spicks. Wo *tong* would handle distribution. But we had to have *money*, man, or the *tong* would just push us out. The Lottery thing was *perfect*. We could set up a *major* refinery. Plus you can hide a *lot* of extra cash behind a big win like that. I was fucking set for *life*."

"And Tyrell?"

His face darkened in the howling red light. He clung to the fence stubbornly, jerking himself back and forth on it as his muscles twitched. "Fucking Steve was out of *control*. But he had a weak heart. I just made sure he had a supply. I had *plans*, you know?"

The wind whistled angrily around my ears. I knew. Damn me, I knew. If I'd only had the sense to wipe Tyrell's message tape before I'd left. But I'd been in a hurry, and Sarah's message had stayed. "Plans. Yeah. Like the massacre at Chaos."

Clinging to the fence, he scrabbled at the ground with his legs, trying to keep away from me. But his grin was wide and wild in the wind. "Wo *tong* was ripe on that. But they got wiped. They're fucking *pissed* at me, man. I didn't tell 'em *you'd* be there. And I guess some blonde whore vaped a dozen by herself. They're ready to take my little *plant*, man."

The scrabbling intensified as the shaking started again. His heart must be a solid bruise by now. Delirium and psychosis were setting in, as evinced in his jerky speech and paranoia. But at least the paranoia was justified. Somebody *was* out to get him.

I lurched forward, reaching to yank him off the fence. The wind howled. "Don't worry about the plant," I gritted. "It won't be here. And neither will you."

AAAAIIIE! Shit, he'd been planning this moment. He'd been shoving the springy fence back like a slingshot. Now, despite his injured legs, he rocketed forward a banshee missile, slamming into me with fists driven by berserker fury. The bullets in his legs didn't even slow him down.

I got a fist in the face that practically snapped my neck, and his teeth sank into my ear. Blood gushed in the wind. I tried to swing the machine gun around, but a flailing foot kicked it away. So I settled for a hard right to the sternum and a left to the ribs.

He staggered away and fell again, his damaged legs giving way. Unfortunately, he was within reach of the Steyr. He dived for it, bringing it up fast. I kicked the muzzle skyward as he fired, and the blasting stream of bullets tore upward through the wind toward the blood-red moon.

Wrenching the gun away by the smoking muzzle, I clubbed him twice across the face with the butt. He rolled, then curled up in a fetal ball, wailing.

"God, God, okay, I *surrender*, okay!?" He scrabbled the crumpled ticket from his pocket and held it out. The wind rattled it in his fingers. "Here, you fucker, *take* it! Just take all the money and *go*! It's what you *want*, right?"

I took the ticket and held it up. It was clear enough in the red moonlight. But I couldn't see it. All I saw was red. Red hair, blowing in the wind. Red lips, kissing my cheek. And red blood, pouring from a small face that only looked sad.

"No," I said, and opened my hand. The red wind blew the damned thing away into the Santa Ana night.

31

I left him inside the plant, sitting on the floor, hands tied behind his back. There was a fifty-five gallon drum of ether sitting behind him, the lid on but not fastened. There was also a gallon drum, loosely capped, balanced on a two-by-four that had one end on the edge of the big drum.

The other end was sitting on top of Magrina's head. His eyes had glared at me with furious heat.

"I thought you killed people in their sleep, you fucking coward," he'd said.

"Oh, I do," I'd admitted. "But that's for clients. You killed my client. So in your case, I'm making an exception."

I'd piled a bunch of scrap lumber, old newspaper and broken furniture around the small vat of crystal meth. The rock-candy "ice" glimmered like rubies in the scarlet moonlight that shone through the broken industrial windows. "See, this time, I'm going to help you stay awake."

I'd sparked a match on my thumb, dropping it into the newspapers beneath the pile. They'd caught quickly, flames rising into the wood, which crackled.

Over the sound of the wind, I'd been able to hear the crystals hiss. Fifty pounds of crystal meth, all cooking at once. It would give Magrina quite a ride, as I'd pointed out to him.

"Of course, if you try to move, or your heart stops and you fall over – the can of ether spills," I'd said. "The flames will set it off, and the drum will go up, which will set off the others. There won't be much left of you but a grease spot. Which is still too much."

"You fucking coward!" Trying his last shot. They all tried this one. "This is chickenshit! I don't have a chance!"

"You have one." My smile had been easy. "You can drop the can now and we'll both die." I'd grinned. "If you have the nerve. I could do it, no problem. Can you?"

He'd just stared at me for a long time. The methedrine fumes were rising thickly from the vat now. Then he'd suddenly snarled.

"Fuck you, you bastard! Just fuck you! I'm *glad* she's dead! I fucked her and killed her and I don't care! So fuck you!"

He'd still kept the can upright, though.

I'd just stepped quietly to the door. The speed was filling the room and I could hear him wheezing deeply.

I don't like drug dealers.

The gravel truck was waiting where I'd left it, outside the gate. The wind howled around me as I climbed into the cab and started the engine. Leaving the windows down, I let the angry wind blow through the cab as I pulled ponderously out onto the dirt road. It was a lot better riding in the cab than in the back.

I rumbled away toward the distant highway. Behind the truck, I saw a flare of yellow light, then another. A second later, twin *BOOMS!* rattled the truck's rickety panels. I didn't even look back.

But by the time I got to the highway, the wind was gone.

SATURDAY

32

Agent Gordon let me into the room with a tight-lipped air. "Five minutes, L'Hiboux. Then I don't owe you shit. Four minutes from now, I'm coming back with a squad. If you're still here, you're under arrest."

I waved at him absently, not really listening. There, in the hospital bed, bathed in the golden sunlight streaming through the curtained window, was a familiar crimson mop.

"Hi." Sarah's voice was a little weak, but still melodious. And her smile was a welcoming dazzle. "Come to get your sleeves back?"

"If you're done with them." I limped forward, a little unsteadily. My eyes and throat felt funny, a little itchy, and I couldn't see too well. But I took the folded sleeve of bulletproof Kevlar fabric from the slim brown hands that had been holding them out. I coughed.

"I almost fell down when I saw the newspaper article. Are . . . you going to be all right?"

The redhead nodded, the smile sweet but tired. "The bullets hit hard enough to punch my broken rib through my lung, but the doctors fixed it. The FBI guy, Gordon, got me here in time. It'll be a couple more weeks."

"Now I owe *him* one," I muttered. Then I took a deep breath, looking at her small tan face tucked against the pillows. She'd never looked prettier. Just like a little girl. I stumbled, trying to find tender words. I found them.

"Well, you were a pain in the ass," I said. And grinned. "But I'm glad you're alive. I had a reputation to keep."

The green eyes studied me seriously. "Jason?"

"I thought you were dead," I said.

She nodded slowly, accepting it. "I would have been." There was a moment's pause, and then she looked back at me. "And the—?"

"Gone," I said. "The wind blew it away."

She tried to shrug, but winced and nodded instead. "I guess it's best. I'll be okay, anyway." Her face suddenly had a faint flush of excitement. "Some producer from RCA was at Linoleum that night and heard me sing. He's already called me twice. He wants to make some test recordings as soon as I'm out of here. He seems really enthusiastic and nice."

"Just watch yourself," I said sternly.

Her face clouded stubbornly. "You're not my dad."

"That's no excuse." I checked my watch. "I'm on a limit here. You have someplace to go?"

She nodded. "My aunt says I can stay with her. She's pretty cool. I'll be okay. Right now I'm just glad to be alive."

"So am I," I said, standing. I felt like I wanted to say something, but I only had a few seconds left. I didn't know Gordon well, but I can spot a man of his word when I meet one. If I was here when he got back, he'd arrest me, no question. And I was tired of fighting for a while. "I've got to go."

Her voice stopped me at the door. "Owl? Not even a kiss goodbye?"

I looked back and grinned. She was giving me the sexiest pout I'd ever seen; all soft puckered lips and demure eyes. She'd go places in the entertainment world, all right. I could feel my Levis getting tight in the crotch again.

"Don't call me Owl," I said, and left.

As I lurched into the stairwell, the elevator down the hall dinged. Agent Gordon and two other suits got off, looking determined. I let the door shut quietly behind me and went down the stairs at a painful run.

But I was grinning.

33

The sky over Western Avenue was as blue as an iris and dotted with fleecy clouds. Though I couldn't see them, I knew the Hollywood Hills would be filled with professional postcard photographers, all jockeying for space. Los Angeles doesn't get perfect skies like that too often. Just after a Santa Ana blows away all the smog.

I limped slowly away from the hospital, basking a bit in the sunshine and trying to sort out my position. The police were probably still looking for me, and they had put an unflattering composite sketch of myself in yesterday's *Times*. I had a couple of bullet holes and a ·223 slug in me, and they'd need medical attention sometime soon. I also had no office at the moment and was at least temporarily out of business.

Oh, well. On the plus side, Sandoval's death and the FBI onslaught on his organization had pretty much eliminated the whole mob. The price was off my head, since there was no one left to pay it. Magrina was dead and Sarah was alive. So was I, for that matter. And there was one other minor plus.

I pulled a rumpled piece of paper worth thirty-eight million dollars from my pocket. The gesture in the desert had been a good one, but the ticket had gotten caught against the cyclone fencing of the plant gate. I'd found it again when I'd brought the truck out. And I wasn't stupid enough to toss it away again without witnesses to be impressed.

"Owl!" The voice was a cheery greeting. I reacted in a panic, practically losing the ticket again as I reached for my gun. But the voice had belonged to the dark, curvacious young girl who was waving at me from the small cafe just ahead. I glowered at her.

"Rosa. *Cómo estás?*"

"You, I must thank." She caught me by the arm and swung me into the small cafe, pointing over the cash register. A clipped-out headline from the *Times* was mounted on the wall. REPUTED DRUGLORD SLAIN IN PARK BATTLE it read, and there were plenty of gory details about just how gruesomely Enrique Sandoval had died.

"You will have coffee? I make good." I noticed that Rosa had underlined a few particularly luscious descriptions of Sandoval's passing. "Yeah. Sure." I decided it wouldn't be a good idea to make her mad. She poured the coffee into a styrofoam cup and handed it to me. I sipped. It was good. "How much?"

She looked insulted. "*Nada!* I would not charge you . . . "

"Rosa!" A chubby cook stepped out from behind the kitchen partition. His hair was slick and greasy. "Back to work! *Pronto!*" He pointed at me. "And make sure that bum pays!"

Rosa looked at me, her eyes reflecting scared apology. "*Lo siento, señor Owl.* Fifty cents. I cannot afford to lose my job . . . I have much family in Salvador. They hope to someday come, if I can—"

"Stow it," I grumbled curtly. I dug two quarters from my pocket and placed them on the counter – using them to weight down a rumpled square of paper.

"Welcome to L.A." I winked at her over the coffee cup and limped out of the store. From the corner of my eye, I could see her lift the ticket curiously. Then her eyes got big. I lurched away.

Across the street I saw a man watching me. A small, hard man, who looked like he was made of stone. His face was impassive, but he nodded once.

I grinned and flipped him off, then turned my back and walked away around the corner of Western and 3rd. The coffee in the cup was the best I ever tasted. The sky was gorgeous. The day was almost perfect. But I knew one way to make it better.

I stopped at a phone booth and rested the coffee cup

on top, digging in my pockets. Down to my last quarter again – but it would be enough. I dropped it in the machine and dialled.

Danny's warm voice answered on the second ring.

"Hey, babe," I said. "Ever been to Tahiti?"

MORE FICTION TITLES AVAILABLE FROM
HODDER & STOUGHTON PAPERBACKS

BOB FORWARD

☐ 51572 9   The Owl   £3.50

LESLIE ALAN HORVITZ

☐ 53216 X   Causes Unknown   £4.50

TERENCE STRONG

☐ 38310 0   Conflict of Lions   £3.50
☐ 41089 2   Dragonplague   £2.99
☐ 32120 2   The Fifth Hostage   £3.50
☐ 50708 X   That Last Mountain   £4.50
☐ 27908 7   Whisper Who Dares   £3.50

All these books are available at your local bookshop or newsagent, or can be ordered direct from the publisher. Just tick the titles you want and fill in the form below.

Prices and availability subject to change without notice.

HODDER AND STOUGHTON PAPERBACKS, P. O. Box 11, Falmouth, Cornwall.

Please send cheque or postal order, and allow the following for postage and packing:

U.K. – 80p for one book, plus 20p for each additional book ordered up to a £2.00 maximum.

B.F.P.O. – 80p for the first book, plus 20p for each additional book.

OVERSEAS INCLUDING EIRE – £1.50 for the first book, plus £1.00 for the second book, and 30p for each additional book ordered.

Name ....

Address ....

....